INFERNO

YOLANDA OLSON

INFERNO SERIES

Inferno Series by Yolanda Olson

Inferno

Cinere

Sparks

Embers

Incendiary

A New Beginning

Scorched

by Yolanda Olson & Jennifer Bene

INFERNO SERIES

Inferno Series by Yolanda Olson

Inferno

Cinere

Sparks

Embers

Incendiary

A New Beginning

Scorched

by Yolanda Olson & Jennifer Bene

BLURB

I don't know where he lost his way,
but we've been made to pay the
price.
To bear the burden of his ... love.
A sickening feeling stirs deep inside
each time he looks at me because I
know what it means.
I have to follow the rules; be his good
girl.
It's the only way to survive in this
house.
Being in the dark never scared me,
being alone was something I used to
cherish until he began to use it
against me.

Against us.

I just want to find the light now.

The place where I know his darkness

can't reach.

A place where maybe everything will

make sense one day, but for now, I

have to be strong.

I won't fall down again.

I can't.

Not before I find my peace there.

I have to do it soon because I'm not

sure how much more I can take.

PROLOGUE

Everything makes sense now.

Why I'm here.

Why it had to be *me* and no one else.

I'm okay with it; as okay as I can be, anyway. I don't want anyone else to have to go through what I am enduring, so I'll gladly take everything he has to offer and praise him the way he tells me to.

Things are easier when I just comply with what he wants. He doesn't do me harm that way, and I even get food when I'm good.

I shake my head as I bring my

dirty, bruised knees up to my chest and hug them close. He says when it's over I'll be canonized and that I'm doing this for the greater good, but I'm convinced he doesn't know what good is. It's so misconstrued that I sometimes wonder if he can tell the difference between reality and fantasy.

But it's okay.

I'm okay.

I'm used to the way things are and I'll make sure that, no matter what happens, he'll be happy. And in turn, I'll still be of use. Not that I really do much but stand and kneel when he tells me to. He says it helps him with what he needs to achieve, and I don't question him. I just do as I'm told, and you would too if you could see his eyes go dark and cold when we enter his special rooms.

I've never been afraid of much before him, and I can honestly say that after being here for the years he's chosen to keep me, the only thing that scares me is telling him no.

That brings the worst kind of repercussion, and the weight of having disappointed him. Solitude and darkness for seven days and seven nights until he's had time to cleanse himself of my negativity. That's how he explains it: *a cleansing*.

Being alone was something I used to love and look forward to; now it's something that terrorizes me more than anything he could ever say when he puts on his displays.

I think I'm on day six of darkness now. I can't remember because every-thing just blends together after a while; time, tears, blood. Each time I'm dumped into this fucking hole, I come closer to losing the will to live. But I come out stronger each time. I don't want to disappoint him, and if I just lay down and died, it would be the biggest disservice in his eyes.

Besides, I haven't come this far,

survived *this* much, just to fucking fall down dead. I don't have it in me to quit, and I have to make him proud.

The gate at the top of the makeshift dungeon opens and, shortly after, a shaky ladder made of rugged rope drops in. It must be the seventh day if I'm being presented with this gesture of freedom.

But I know that this is a treason punishable by death unless Pater has given permission for any of us to be removed from the oubliette.

Pater.

That is not his name but rather a title that he requires we address him by. He's earned it, he says, for putting up with us, for choosing to care for us in his own special way, and for all the years he spent studying his rituals.

I know his real name because he's whispered it into my ear during nights of unwanted lust and pain. I've survived as long as I have because I know that pleasure for him is not just physical; seducing his thoughts is the only way to stay alive, and even on nights when I wished that Hell would open and swallow me whole, I refused to leave the boys behind. I've stepped into their pain more than once to save them from things they shouldn't understand at such young ages, things they should never have to experience unless it's something they want, and he sees me as a prize for doing so.

I fear the day he gets bored with me though, because then there will be nothing left I can do to keep them as safe as I can. It's why I try my best to please him, to keep him happy any way I can, because nights spent down in the oubliette leaves them free to be tortured and fucked against their will.

With the strength I've managed to hold onto, I get up from the dirty, cold rocky ground, and walk over to the ladder. It's only being anchored by the strength of whomever is holding it, and I pray that it's the older of the two. He's the only one who can bear the strain of someone bigger than him, and if he doesn't hold on, the ladder will fall and send me back down toward a sure death.

If it were just me in this situation, then fine; let the ladder fall, let me die, but goddammit. I have to keep them safe, and I have to get the fuck out of here to do that. I have to watch my mouth, I have to not speak back to Pater, and I have to do as he wishes at all times. If I don't, I'll know that the next time I'm in the oubliette, the others will suffer terribly, and it will be on my soul.

I *refuse* to die a failure. I *refuse* to allow them such a fate alone when I know that my part in this is simple, and I just have to learn to accept it.

When he took me from my previous life, he told me he'd chosen me to be his wife; he'd even preformed some kind of ceremony to solidify this in his own mind, because

I know that nothing we do here will be seen as such in the eyes of the law or anything above or below.

A hand firmly grips mine as I reach the top, shaking me from the thoughts of what I know I must do, but have so much trouble abiding by. In a matter of seconds, I'm looking into the solemn, brown eyes of Vaughn. He's lost a lot of the light and luster he had when he first arrived here and I can understand why, but beneath the solemnness I can see a sense of urgency, and I know that my early freedom was not orchestrated by Pater, but rather out of necessity.

With a final grunt, he pulls me over the top and begins to roll up the ladder as I start the long sprint back toward the house. I won't wait for Vaughn; I can't. If I do, Pater will know I was helped out of my prison and that will put Vaughn in danger. Instead, I'll just tell him I clawed my way out when he asks. I've been known to make it halfway to the top before breaking my nails as I slide all the way back down again.

He's seen me do it with his own eyes the first time he lowered me into this sensory deprived hell. But Pater is a complicated man and likes to see things as they are presented in the moment.

He'll believe me.

He *has* to believe me.

Because if he doesn't, we all die.

CHAPTER ONE

What I stumble upon when I enter Pater's home as I'm trying to frantically control my breathing is not what I expected from the urgency in Vaughn's eyes. The waiting room is empty, the living room just as hollow, and there are no trails of blood or anything hinting toward punishment on his dusty wooden floors.

So then why set me free ahead of schedule?

A silent answer is my reward when I turn in time to see him running up the long walkway toward the still open door. He puts a finger to his lips before leaning down and attempting to collect himself. I know he's scared, and I know that this must be important.

He tosses the neatly gathered rope toward the door and beckons for me to follow him. I trust him enough to blindly fall into step behind him, though I can't help but feel uneasy about where he's leading me.

Vaughn never has much to say these days. He lives in his own world most of the time, and he usually only ever comes to life when I'm around because he knows of my need to protect them. He does the same for me in his own way. Whenever I've been tossed into the little part of the world where Pater can forget about me for a week at a time, he sneaks out and drops scraps of food through the small cracks of the door.

It's not much, it never is, but it's enough to keep me alive and from starving to death as I think Pater wants for me sometimes. I don't know why he would want such a fate for someone he's taken as his "wife", but he has his reasons.

Maybe one day we'll find out what they are. Or maybe we'll die in the dark, confused as to what this all truly stood for.

As we near the opulent kitchen area where Pater eats like a fucking king, Vaughn turns to look at me and presses a finger slowly to his lips. A few steps later, we're both peeking around the door frame and now I understand why I was taken prematurely from my punishment.

Pater is leaning against the counter, his arms crossed loosely over his chest, with Eloy sitting in a stool. I roll my eyes at how pristine he looks and how we always look like we're mired in shit.

Eloy is the youngest of the three of us. He's thirteen and, for the moment, he's dressed as cleanly and beautifully as Pater. I hear the voice of someone I don't recognize and crane my neck to see if I can get a better look, but Vaughn pulls me back just as Pater's eyes start to wander in our direction.

"Get cleaned up," he whispers in his soft voice. "We have to go in and speak to that lady."

And as he walks into the kitchen, leaving me in the hallway, it's the first time I noticed since being pulled out of the pit that he's dressed like a prince, too. I'm the only one who looks like I've been through Hell, because I have.

A wide smile stretches over Pater's face as he sees Vaughn entering the room.

"And this is my other son," I can hear him say. I cringe at those words. *My other son.* If only this person who we're being presented to knew what kind of man Pater is, what kind of woman he forces me to be, she would take Vaughn and Eloy and run.

I could tell her.

I could weave a powerful tale of the horrors we face here, the things we're forced to endure, the evil man that Pater is, but I won't. If she doesn't believe me—and who would believe such a fantastical story—I go back into the oubliette permanently.

I sigh as I run toward the other end of the house. We are not allowed upstairs unless Pater requests our company because it's his home, and he deems that his personal space. It's how he keeps us separate from what he calls his 'normal' life, though there are times when he'll invite me upstairs, but never the boys.

That I know of, anyway. The only thing I ever pray for anymore is that they have never been forced to go with him into his room. They know they can trust me and tell me if they have, but I never broach the subject because they're afraid of me.

Not as much as they're afraid of Pater, but they're still afraid.

I don't blame them.

I would also fear the person that's supposed to be like a mother to me, who instead decides to carry out painful and sometimes erotic punishments as directed to her in the most terrible ways.

This is why I know I never want to bear children of my own. If this is what I'm forced to do—to actually be capable of putting them through—then the only thing I truly deserve is a slow death at their hands.

But they fear me and will never raise a hand against me because I'm the only person who knows their pain and torture. I'm the only person that would believe them, and I'm the only person that can keep them as safe as possible from Pater.

I take their places as often as I can, but there are even nights when I'm so physically and mentally exhausted from the constant torrent of abuse that I can't save them. I believe that those are the nights that their hatred for me grows, and the fear begins to slowly drift away.

If they did end up killing me, I would not blame or despise them for the deed. I would only hope that they allow me the opportunity to send Pater to Hell before me.

What do I wear? I don't even know who that woman is.

Pater, Vaughn, and Eloy were dressed casually but a little more presentable than normal when we have guests, so I assume she's of enough importance for me to wear a dress.

I just have to find one long enough to cover the scratches on my knees.

Pulling open the closet doors, I begin to quickly pick through my choices.

"I've always liked this one the best."

My body freezes under the

weight of his breath, hot on my ear. One hand reaches forward and retrieves a blue and white floral sundress, while the other gently rests on my side.

He could crush me right now between his hands if he wanted to, but then he would have no wife to present to the woman in the kitchen.

"You know that as soon as she leaves you're going back in." It's a statement, not a question, but I expected nothing less.

I nod as he lets his lips rest gently on my neck. "Maybe I'll fuck you before I throw you back. Or maybe I'll punish you a little more. Decisions, decisions."

"Whatever you desire, Pater," I reply quietly. That's the answer he likes the best, and I'm only here to maintain a happy home for him, which means he has to be happy as well.

"I don't think I'll ever get sick of fucking you," he whispers as he reaches down and begins to push my torn, dirty panties off.

I take a deep breath and use every ounce of bravery I have to gently push his hands away.

"We have a visitor, Pater. She must be important if you need me to be present. I shouldn't keep her waiting," I say softly.

He grunts in annoyance, but he knows I'm right. Besides, the last thing I want right now is to have to lie on the bed while he uses me for however long he wants to. It's fucking degrading that I have to be so subservient to him, but it's how I stay alive. I'm willing to do it for as long as I need to be able to gain a safe escape for Eloy and Vaughn.

"Don't forget to cover that shit up," he warns, nodding at the cuts on my legs.

"Yes Pater," I reply unhappily.

"Hey," he says, turning me to face him and sliding his arms around my waist. Pater is a tall man so I'm staring unhappily into his chest, but he leans down to look into my eyes, cocking his head to the side so I can see his smile.

"I'm almost done with three of you. This won't go on for much longer, then I'll let you decide if you want to stay or go, okay? Smile for me, pretty baby," he says as I glance up slowly into his golden brown eyes.

The stubble on his face is black and has some gray in it, matching his hair perfectly. He looks so fucking normal, like a loving father, but I know better.

We know better.

I force a smile on my face, which makes him stand back up to his full height and kiss me on the forehead.

"That's my girl. Now get yourself cleaned up and come down as quick as you can. And keep that smile on your face; we're a perfectly happy family and I want her to know it."

I nod again, turn, and grab the dress he picked out, and head toward the dresser. Once I've picked out some fresh underwear, I quickly make my way toward the bathroom and lock the door firmly behind me.

Fuck.

At least it'll be over soon.

CHAPTER TWO

Twenty minutes later, I'm rushing down the hallway. Normally, after a week in the oubliette, my showers last for at least an hour, but I know I don't have enough time for that. As I round the corner into the kitchen, I quickly reach down and smooth out the hem of my dress, before plastering a huge smile on my face.

"There she is," Pater says, holding out an arm toward me.

"I'm so sorry I'm late," I reply brightly as I obediently walk over to him. He leans down and kisses me on the lips. It's a firm kiss and far from gentle, but it's hard for him to pretend he's something he's not.

"Laura, this is my wife, Jocelyn," he says, holding me close against him.

"Pleasure to meet you," she says with a warm smile.

"Likewise! Can I get you anything? Coffee? Water? Juice?" I ask, trying to remember what Pater lets me offer on the very rare occasion we have company.

"No thank you," she says, crossing her arms, the top of the island separating her from the boys. "I'm just about done talking to them, then I'd like to speak to the two of you privately."

"Oh, of course!"

Pater tightens his grip on me. Apparently, my acting is lacking today, but I was just in a fucking hole in the ground for six days. I'm hoping he'll cut me some slack when she leaves - instead of just cutting *me*.

"Would you like to wrap up with them without us here?" Pater asks Laura.

"Actually, that would be great!" she replies with an enthusiastic nod.

"Alright, we'll be just down the hallway then. One of you boys can bring her to the living room when you're done in here, okay?" he says, walking over and putting a firm hand on each of their shoulders.

"I will," Vaughn replies quietly, looking up at him.

Pater smiles at him and nods, before he turns and holds his hand out toward me. Without hesitation, I take it and let him lead me out of the kitchen, but I cast one last glance over my shoulder at the trio. Vaughn is speaking quietly to Laura, and Eloy glances at me with wide eyes. I shake my head once before I disappear from sight.

"So, who is she?" I ask Pater curiously as we head down the hallway.

"We'll talk about that after she leaves," he replies in an even tone.

Oh God, this can't be good.

"Okay," I agree softly.

Once we reach the living room, he walks over toward the window and pulls the curtain back. I watch him as he glances around until his eyes land on something and narrow. I won't question him anymore. I don't even plan on speaking unless spoken to at this point. Something has Pater very angry, and my leg is already shaking in anticipation of what it could possibly be.

Silence.

That's the only thing that sits heavily in the air between us as he walks away from the window and falls into the spot next to me on the couch. He has nothing else to say to me because, by all rights, I shouldn't even be in his sights until tomorrow night.

Pater irritably runs a hand over

his mouth and crosses his arms behind his head.

"What the fuck could they possibly be talking about?" he mutters.

I don't respond. I know he wasn't speaking to me, and in his state of current anger, a response would most likely result in additional correction.

"It was so nice to meet the two of you."

Laura's voice finally echoes through the hallway as she's led to us. "Remember, if you ever need anything, you can call me and I'll do my best to help, okay?"

"Okay. Thank you," Vaughn's dejected voice responds. "Our parents should be in there. It was nice to meet you, too."

A few seconds later, Laura enters the room. Pater gets to his feet to greet her, and I stay right where I am as she settles onto the couch across from us.

"You have wonderful sons. You

must be very proud of them," she says brightly, taking a small notebook out of her purse.

"We are," Pater replies.

"Speaking of children," she says, turning her attention toward me, "Exactly how old are you? You don't look old enough to be their mother."

My body immediately begins to shake. My mouth opens and closes a couple of times, but nothing comes out.

"Old enough to have children," Pater says, putting an arm around my shoulder and giving me a reassuring squeeze.

Even if they're not mine.

"I'm sorry if I sounded intrusive. I was just hoping to get some beauty tips," Laura jokes, as she flips her notebook open and then produces a pen. "I just have a couple of questions for you, and then I'll be on my way."

"Fire away," he says, with that charming grin sitting on his face.

"Well, Eloy and Vaughn seem like sullen, but happy children. Are they usually like that?" she asks.

Pater squeezes my arm. He doesn't know how to answer the question, because he's never been near them unless it's for some kind of sadistic need.

"Vaughn usually doesn't have much to say; he's the quiet studious type, you know? And Eloy hasn't been feeling well lately so that could explain his mood," I say, leaning forward and clasping my hands in my lap.

She nods in understanding as she jots something down in her notebook.

"How are their studies?"

"Great! Like I said, Vaughn likes to learn things. He's very curious about how things work and if there's meaning behind every function. I expect him to be a scientist or something similar," I reply with a smile. "Eloy. Now, he likes his sports and he's happiest when he's outside exploring, so he's kind of like his brother in that respect."

Laura looks at me with a pleased smile on her face. Apparently, my answers are what she wants to hear, when I'm really just telling her the truth. I do teach them when I'm not in the fucking hole, and I try to make sure they understand basic educational studies.

"And my last question is actually about the two of you. I would like if you could both answer me," she says, giving Pater a pointed glance. "How are things? Any worries you have that you may want to share with me? I'm not here to judge you, please understand that. I'm here out of concern and I want to make sure that you're both as equally happy as your children."

"Concern?" I ask her in confusion.

She smiled warmly. "I'll address that in a moment; first, I'd like to know how things are."

"Honestly, I couldn't be happier. Are things perfect? No, of course not. Perfection is a lie, an illusion. But my husband provides for us as best as he can and makes sure that we're well taken care of. I can't think of anything else I could possibly want," I reply with a shrug. *Except for you to take us with you when you leave.*

"Yeah, I agree. My wife maintains a tidy home as you can see. She keeps our boys educated and I don't think we've ever really had an argument. Any disagreements we actually have had have never been in front of our children, so I think we're doing okay," he adds, rubbing my back affectionately.

"Great!" Laura says as she jots what I assume to be her final thoughts about her trip into her notebook. I wait patiently, trying to still my jumping leg as she places her notebook back into her purse and looks up at us.

"So let me tell you the reason for

my visit," she says, looking from me to Pater. His hand comes to rest in the middle of my back, almost as if he's expecting her to say it was *my* fault, so he could pull my spine out.

"For obvious reasons, any calls placed to me are anonymous, but I had a concerned parent reach out to me recently. It seems that Eloy has been spotted out in the woods behind your home, killing small animals. As a matter of fact, the parent that called me stated that they witnessed him skinning a snake and then attempting to eat it."

I lean back in shock, but Pater chuckles almost immediately. "Aren't snakes considered a delicacy somewhere around the world? What's the harm in it? He's just being a kid."

Closing my eyes, I decide it's best to let him handle this conversation because, judging by his response, I can tell that anything that comes out of his mouth next will be dripping with sugar. The only question I have remaining is whether Laura will buy it.

Well, maybe more than one question...

"Where did you say you were from again?" I asked her suspiciously.

"Oh, I'm just another concerned parent. I'm not tied to any official agency," she says nervously.

"Then what the fuck are you doing in our home? When *my* son comes to *your* house and tries to skin and eat *you,* then you have my fucking permission to show up with 'concern.' Until then, you can get the fuck out of here!" I shout, jumping to my feet. My fists are balled at my sides, and I can't remember the last time I have ever been so angry.

Laura's mouth jumps open at my sudden outburst, but Pater laughs in appreciation. I'm not protective over many things in this world, because I really don't have anything, but those boys are my heart, and he knows I would kill for them.

"I think you should listen to my wife," he says, as he rises from the couch to stand next to me. "And tell your 'concerned parent friends' that they can come over and talk to us about our kids anytime they want. Tell them we'll be waiting with an open door and a smile on our faces, because our boys are well fed, happy, cared for, and that's all that matters to us."

Laura nervously gets to her feet and nods, but as she begins to walk past us on her way toward the front door, something inside me tells me that if she makes it out, our entire family will be in danger.

And that's why when I grab the lamp off the corner table and follow her toward the door, I know Pater will let me put her in the oubliette in my place.

Because while she's now stumbling from the blow to her head, trying to stay on her feet, he knows what's in my heart. And he'll allow me to do everything I can for Eloy and Vaughn, even though I know he has to punish them first.

CHAPTER THREE

"Why did you let her in?" I asked him as I begin to drag her back down toward the back door. "Did she show you some credentials?"

"Nah. I just thought it could be fun to fuck with the neighbors," he replies with a smirk. "I knew she wasn't anyone important. And you should be thankful I let her in. It got you out of the hole for a while and into a nice dress. As a matter of fact, a 'thank you, Pater' would actually be nice, instead of your bitching."

"Thank you, Pater," I say through gritted teeth. I take a deep breath and stand up straight for a moment when the sudden severity of what I've done hits me.

"Oh shit. Oh *fuck*," I say frantically. "I can't believe I did that."

"It's 'cause you want to protect our little family as much as I do," he chuckles. "That's why you're my favorite of all the wives I've had. You would do anything to keep our secret and our boys safe, wouldn't you?"

"Yes," I reply softly.

"None of my other wives gave two shits about any kids we had. They all just wanted to fuck and stay out of the oubliette. It always got so boring. You, on the other hand," he says, walking toward me and taking my face in between his strong hands, "couldn't care less about fucking me. You're more invested in being a good mother, and *that's* why I appreciate you as much as I do. Now, if we could just do something about that mouth, maybe you wouldn't spend so much time in the ground."

It's the oddest feeling that's taken over me right now. Pride because of the praise I'm receiving as a mother, but anger because of the fact that I can't protect them as much as I want to.

Pater narrows his eyes and smirks, "I can't tell if that's a scowl on your face or a smile, so I'll just assume it's a little bit of both and be okay with it."

Laura moves next to us on the ground and begins her attempt to get to her feet, but I'm sure I hit her hard enough to keep her down a little while longer.

"What am I going to do with her?" I ask him quietly.

"Well. You got two choices. You can finish whatever it was you started..."

"Or?" I ask him, wringing my hands.

"I don't think you're going like this, but I think it could be fun," he says, flashing me his wide grin. I raise an eyebrow and wait. If he wants to fuck her, that's his prerogative, obviously, but I'm not joining in.

"Eloy!"

His voice booms throughout the house so unexpectedly that I jump in surprise and almost losing my footing.

"What are you doing?" I ask him curiously.

"Did you just ask me a question?" he asks, tilting his head, the grin widening on his face.

"No, Pater."

"I didn't think so," he says, turning his attention toward the sound of footsteps quickly approaching. "Hey there, son."

"Hello," Eloy replies nervously.

"I didn't know you liked to skin animals," Pater says conversationally. "I used to be into that when I was a kid, too. I figure we could have a little bonding moment if you're up for it. And to sweeten the deal, if you say yes to what I'm going to suggest, I'll

38

make sure your mom doesn't have to serve the rest of her time in the oubliette."

Eloy's eyes widen hopefully as he glances quickly in my direction. He knows that the more time I spend *above* ground, the less time him and his brother are off Pater's radar.

"I agree," he immediately says.

Pater throws his head back and laughs. He knows that the boys need me as much as I need them, and that they'll do anything to keep me above ground.

"Good. Then what I want for you to do is drag that piece of shit out back. Hit her as many times as you need to keep her quiet. I'll be out shortly. I just wanna finish talking with your mom," he says to him as he glances at me.

"Okay," he agrees, grabbing Laura by her hands and dragging her the rest of the way out of the house. A feeling of dread quickly cascades over me when it starts to set in. I have a terrible feeling that I know how he plans on bonding with Eloy.

"Listen, I can tell you've already got this figured out by the look on your face, but there's something I want to tell you. I feel like I owe it to you for being such a good mom," he says, rubbing his chin thoughtfully.

"Don't hurt him," I beg, reaching forward and grabbing his forearms. "I can talk to him and tell him to be more careful. Please?"

Pater looks down at my hands and waits for me to pull them away before he responds. "We'll see what happens, alright? But I do need to punish him for being so fucking sloppy. You understand," he says with a wink as he starts to make his way outside.

I run to the door as he closes it behind him and crack it open. He probably heard the door open again, because he shakes his head as he walks toward the woods.

I find myself secretly hoping that

whoever saw Eloy skinning and eating the snake will catch Pater doing whatever the hell it is he has planned - but I also hope they don't. My son shouldn't be punished for behaving like an animal, since that's how he's pretty much been brought up under Pater. He's only behaving as he's been taught, the way his father has conditioned him to. And for that, a nosy neighbor is going to die, Eloy is going to be "punished", and I have to sit here and hope for his life to be spared.

All because he blindly made a deal to keep me safe. Anything that happens to him will be my fault; Pater made that clear enough when he tricked Eloy by using me as a pawn.

I know I shouldn't do this because we're not allowed to without Pater, but I close the door and run as quickly as I can to the second floor of his home. I'll get a better view of the woods from his bedroom window, and that's how I'll know for sure if anything happens to Eloy.

Or, more painful still, what *will* happen to Eloy. With a lump in my throat and a sickened feeling in my heart, I make my way up the stairs and down to his bedroom door at the end of the hall.

I hope he doesn't see me because if he does, he'll take out his anger on the boy. If he doesn't, I'll know how to avenge Eloy if necessary. When the opportunity presents itself.

CHAPTER FOUR

An eternity.

That's how long I feel like I've been standing here, peeking through his bedroom window without a thing in sight, and I'm so fucking scared.

My husband is out there somewhere in the woods with our son, a nosy neighbor, and enough rage to punish them both with a smile on his face.

But what kind of father would that really make him? To punish his child for doing something that obviously makes him happy would be hypocritical of him, and Pater prides himself on being the very opposite of that.

But where are they? Why is there no sign of life between the trees when I know there are three people somewhere out there in the isolation?

I sigh unhappily and let the curtain drift back over the window again as I sit on the edge of his bed. This is not a place I've ever enjoyed being, and it seems to be more of a hell in the current situation of not knowing.

"Hello?"

My eyes widen as I run out of the room and find Vaughn in the hallway peeking into doors. Neither of us should be up here, but it's more dangerous for him because if Pater gets a whiff of his scent having roamed through his private space, it makes him fair game.

"Go back downstairs *now*," I hiss at him frantically. He stares at me in confusion. He thinks the danger is not real because Pater isn't in the house, but I know better. I fucking know better, and I have to get him back down to where he belongs.

"If he smells you up here, you're going to end up in his room," I say as I walk toward him, grip him firmly by the arm and begin to steer him back toward the stairs. "Get downstairs. Stay there; lock yourself in my room. I'll figure out how to fix this."

"But --"

"Now," I say again, firmly setting him on the staircase. I cross my arms over my chest and glare at him until he reluctantly begins his descent. I hate having to treat Vaughn with such false, overbearing anger, but if he believes he's angered me, he'll listen.

And it will keep him safe.

I don't know how Pater can tell when someone has been upstairs, but my curiosity got the best of me one day when he had been out buying groceries for himself, and I went up to his private floor. He found me later that night, curled up in my room reading a book, and quite literally dragged me all the way back upstairs and into his bedroom.

He told me he had been able to smell me in the place he told us was off limits; that he knew it was me because the hallways smelled of lavender and forgotten innocence. He told me that since I had broken his simplest rule, he had no choice but to break me in return.

I wrap my arms around myself and shiver as memories of that first night in his bed threaten to wash over me and drown me where I stand.

Pater is an evil man in everything he does, and that night was no exception. However, I cannot allow myself to be lost in those thoughts. I have to rid the upstairs of Vaughn's scent, then go back to the window and hope that I'll finally catch a glimpse of Eloy.

It honestly worries me that I'm so invested in being an actual maternal figure to them now more than ever. It means I've accepted Pater as their father and as my husband, but I will do what I must to keep them safe from his misplaced sexual desires. I will take the brunt of his devious needs, and I will make sure they're kept safe from things they shouldn't have forced upon them.

They shouldn't be here, and neither should I, but this is the hand we were dealt, and he chose us specifically for this very reason. At least, that's what he's told me before, though I don't know how much I believe of his story.

As long as it keeps Vaughn and Eloy out of his bedroom and out of his special rooms, I will gladly be the sacrificial lamb. It's what a mother would do, isn't it? Lay down her life for that of her children? I know I'll find out soon enough, but for now I just want some sign that Eloy is alive, and to rid the upper floor of Vaughn's scent.

I've made it as far as his bathroom when I hear the front door of the home open. He's laughing loudly, the echo booming throughout the downstairs of the house, and I know I'm too late. I won't be able to do much to deflect his knowledge that Vaughn transgressed him, but I will still try my damnedest.

But as I leave his bathroom with a can of air freshener in my hand and begin to vigilantly spray the hallway as I run down its length, something slows me down. Pater is still laughing, yet there's no other sound accompanying him. No sound of an upset young boy being mocked or praised, no sound of the additional set of footsteps that *should* have entered in the house with him.

And as he begins to ascend the staircase, I try my best to steady myself against the wall next to me. Is he laughing because of what Eloy has done? Or because of what *he* has done to Eloy?

CHAPTER FIVE

By the time he reaches the top stair, I've saturated the hallway as best as I can and I'm standing in a choking fog of ocean breeze. I don't care that he'll see me here, as long as I've done my part to keep Vaughn off his fucking radar.

He stops when he sees me standing just beyond the landing and his laughter gives way to a grin. I watch as his head tilts to the left and begin to shiver as his eyes travel up and down my body before resting on the can I'm holding.

"What are you doing up here, Jocelyn?" he asks in a quiet, sickening tone.

"I ... I ..."

He chuckles and walks toward me, jerking the air freshener out of my hand and takes a deep breath. He narrows his eyes for a moment and looks behind me before he nods in understanding.

"Bad, bad, bad," he chides, shaking his head slowly. "Why are you all behaving so badly all of a sudden? Do you like being punished?"

The slight bounce in his step tells me that, regardless of my answer, he's going to do whatever he deems necessary to correct my misstep, and I can't fight him over it because it would mean Vaughn would have to take my place.

"Pater?" I begin slowly. "Where's Eloy?"

"Did you ... Did you just ask me

a question?" he inquires in a mocking tone as the grin fades from his rugged face.

Normally, I would back down. I would tell him *no* and I would await whatever punishment he deemed necessary and allow him to take the appropriate corrective steps against me. But Eloy is missing now, and I want fucking answers, no matter the cost.

"Yes," I reply defiantly. "Where is he? Where's the boy?"

Pater walks quickly toward me, and I can feel my body stiffen, but I maintain the defiance in my eyes that I feel in my heart for him as he stops in front of me. His breathing is uneven, and I can see the fire burning in his gaze, but I refuse to let him consume me in those flames; not until I know where Eloy is.

His hand flies through the air and lands firmly across my face, almost knocking me to the ground.

The sting of it makes my eyes water slightly and I stumble, but don't fall. This isn't what he wants. He doesn't want me to oppose him; he's told me that so many times before, and that's why my second home is that abandoned fucking hole in the ground.

I wish I had the will sometimes to not fight him and just let him kill me, but these boys – who would fight for them if I lay down and died?

"Now, I'm going to ask you again," he says in an even tone. "Did you just ask me a question?"

I put my fingers gingerly to my lip and wipe away the blood from the small cut. He's never hit me hard enough to draw blood before, because he cares about my outside appearance. I use my tongue to quickly lick away the copper tasting drops still lingering on the corner of my mouth before I answer him.

"Yes. *Where is the boy?*"

His mouth tightens into an angry line as he stares down at me. He should expect this from me by now when it comes to the welfare of the children, and I find myself wondering if he left his common sense out in the woods as well.

"Let's get a couple of things straight here," he says, after letting out a deep sigh. "First of all, he's not your son. Neither of them are; you're just the stupid little bitch I chose to play mommy to them. What I decide to do with them, or *to* them, is really not your fucking concern. Remember that."

Pater crosses his arms over his chest and the grin begins to return. He likes to use words to cut me down; he always said that words would leave a deeper cut than any blade. Words – the ones spoken to inflict harm – will stay with you much longer than any scar worn on the skin.

If Pater is anything, he's a master of cutting deeply with his words.

Don't let him do this while you still don't know where Eloy is.

"Secondly," he says, dropping his arms to his sides, "You can't keep secrets from me. Even when you think you've got everything figured you, you should know better by now. Which begs a question. You haven't been up here alone, have you? No amount of that shit you sprayed can hide it from me, which means I'll give you an option. Even though you don't deserve it, even though *he* doesn't deserve it, tell me. Who's keeping me company in bed tonight? You, or the nosy little fuck that can't do as he's told?"

"Neither," I reply, my voice wavering slightly. *Fuck. He'll know he's getting to me now.*

Pater runs a hand irritably over his face before he chuckles. "I don't know why you think you have a say in the matter. Now, either you pick, or I will."

I let out an unhappy sigh as I turn and begin to walk back toward his bedroom. He knows that, given the choice, I'll always place myself in harm's way to spare them.

"Not so fast," he says, in a tone that stops me in my tracks.

I don't turn to face him immediately because I'm worried about what it is he wants before he subjects me to the level of correction he feels I deserve for talking back to him. For standing my ground against a tyrant and exercising a basic human right that I was stripped of the moment I willingly walked through his door, because I agreed to be less than human. I agreed to be this empty marionette to do his will and now, after all this time, I find myself rejecting the idea, even though it's too damn late.

"Yes, Pater?" I ask quietly as I finally turn my body toward the wall. It still can be seen as an act of defiance because I'm not facing him completely, but it's enough of a submission that he won't add anything extra to the punishment he's ready to bestow upon me.

"I want you to do a few things for me before I do a few things to *you*," he says, a wicked smile starting to spread across his lips.

"Yes, Pater?" I inquire again curiously. This isn't normally how he does these things, and the worry that has washed over me is being overshadowed with doubt and wonder.

"Let's call this little game *A List of Tasks*. For each task you complete, I'll go a little easier on you tonight. Of course, if you complete them all, you're still going to be punished, but not as severely. Questions?" he asks.

I don't respond. Not verbally, because I've already talked myself into enough shit to have to add more to drown in. Instead, I shake my head and nervously begin to wring my hands while I wait for his first task.

"My God. If only you knew how beautiful you are when you just stand there with your mouth shut," he remarks with a wistful sigh. "Alright. Task number one; it's going to answer your question."

My question?

"The first thing I want you to do is go out into the woods behind the house. Find the mess the boy made and clean it up. I want it so spotless out there you'd never know that anything other than animals shit between those trees. When you're done, you come back up and we'll talk about your next task."

I run past him and damn near fall down the stairs. If he wants me to cover Eloy's tracks, then chances are he's still alive. He may be bruised, battered, and beaten, but he's still alive and now I have the chance to be the mother he deserves and help him.

But I can't shake the chuckle Pater let out when I ran past him, and I know this task won't be as simple as finding some shit to clean up.

Whatever it is I find is going to break my heart, mind, and soul.

CHAPTER SIX

The most damning thing about what Pater has set as his first task is that I know it will easily break me if something has happened to Eloy. If I'm broken, I can no longer fight for them. I don't care about myself; I am disposable because I'm not the first wife he's had, just the one that has survived the longest.

But for Eloy and Vaughn to be left alone in his care again until he decides he wants another wife is more than I can take. It's a weight on my shoulders that's been threatening to crush me for quite some time now, and while my foundation may be slowly crumbling, I will not collapse until they're safe.

I'm my own worst enemy in all of this. My constant fear of failing the children is starting to undo me, and the nights I spend in the oubliette would be much more bearable if I didn't have them to worry about.

I can see him now as I quicken my pace, the grass crushing beneath my feet. I can see Eloy standing naked, almost completely hidden in the brush that leads into the woods. He has marks on his back, and from what I can tell, they aren't severe.

"Eloy!" I call out as I run faster.

His body is shaking; I can see it now the closer I get to him. The marks on his back look like a series of scratches, but I can plainly see where he has been lashed with a switch. I call his name again, but he doesn't turn to face me. Instead, he balls his hands at his sides and lets out a sob.

"I'm here now, it's okay," I promise as I finally reach him and put a hand gently on his shoulder. I guide him into the woods to keep our conversation hidden from any eyes that may be watching. Even though I know we can't be heard out here, I also know he'll use our body language to deduce whatever the fuck he wants and punish us accordingly.

"I'm sorry. I didn't want to. I'm sorry," he wails miserably.

"Nothing we do here is by choice; you know that. Whatever you've done, it was because you were made to. I'm just happy you're okay," I say, trying my best to comfort him, but the fact that he's shaking his head and still refusing to face me destroys any hope that Pater hasn't already defiled him.

I push my way through the brush as I move around to the front of him. His teeth are grinding together, and he lowers his face so that I don't see how much he currently resembles a wounded animal.

"What did you do, Eloy?" I ask gently. I place a hand on either side of his face and pull him toward me. His body is covered with lash marks, and the haunting sound of Pater's malicious laughter when he reentered the house begins to taunt my memories.

"It's okay. I promise. I'm here to help you. I'll fix whatever you've done; you just need to tell me where to go, and I'll fix it."

"I didn't want to. I didn't want to, but he made me do it," he repeats desperately. What could he have been forced to do that's rendered him a babbling mess? I would imagine Laura was already dead by the time they had dragged her out here.

Wasn't she?

"He made me fuck her. He made me do it. I didn't want to and when I refused he started to whip me. Then he told me--" his voice broke into another anguished sob as he buried his face in my hair and finally wrapped his arms around me.

"What did he say? He can't hear us right now, and I swear to you I won't repeat it. What did he say, Eloy?" I press gently as I run a hand softly over his hair.

Eloy takes a small series of deep breaths to try and calm himself, and it works long enough for him to tell me what the price of his refusal was.

"He said that if I didn't fuck her, he would make me fuck you. He said he would make Vaughn watch us and then he would kill us all. I'm sorry," he says, as he resumes his uncontrollable sobbing.

"Don't cry. It's okay, I promise it's okay."

I feel a rage starting to intensify deep within. Pater's sexual appetites are unrivaled, and his devious words are always enough to get us to do what he wants but doing this to Eloy – he's crossed a fucking line, and he knows it. That's why he made me come out here; not to clean up a physical mess but to fix a psychological one he knows I don't have control over.

"Listen very closely to me right now. Eloy? Look at me, please," I say, stepping back and gently removing his arms from around me.

He uses the back of his hand to wipe the tears away from his face, but does as he's requested and locks eyes with me. My heart hurts for him when I look into those beautiful brown eyes. They're so devoid of any meaning - so dead and hopeless that nothing will ever bring life to them again.

"I'm going to help you escape," I say, pulling off my shirt. I quickly wrap it around his waist and tie it securely. "This isn't much, but at least you won't leave as degraded as he's made you. Follow me."

He nods as we walk back toward the line that divides Pater's property from the woods and I glance at the door.

Empty.

Good.

"When I get to the door, I want you to run as fast as you can. Do you understand? Run away from this terrible fucking place. I'll cover for you. I'll tell him that you were far beyond reproach, and I killed you as a mercy. I'll tell him I buried your body under Laura's. He'll believe me. He has to believe me."

With as much as I hate to admit it to myself, killing Eloy would actually be the kinder mercy than letting him run away. He has no chance of a normal life outside of Pater's rule and he won't know where to go, but I have to try.

"Come on, this is our only shot at this. Don't worry about any of us, just fucking run as soon as I get to the door, okay?"

He nods and slowly begins to follow me toward the back of the house. As soon as I reach the door, I turn slightly and nod, but just as Eloy begins to run, an upstairs window opens.

"That's a bad fucking idea, kid."

Nausea quickly overcomes me as I glance up and see Pater at the upstairs window. What makes my blood turn cold, what makes Eloy stop running, is when we see he has Vaughn in the window with him.

"Come on up. It looks like we need to have a family meeting. And you should probably get a move on. I'm getting hard just thinking of all the possibilities," he says, giving me a menacing smile.

"No!"

I push the back door almost off its hinges and begin to run back up to Pater's room. Eloy is behind me. I can hear his feet slapping the floor as he desperately tries to keep up with my frantic pace.

And just as I make it to the top landing, I can hear Vaughn let out a pained scream.

I'm too late.

CHAPTER SEVEN

I damn near end up barreling
through the door, and I would have
been successful had Pater not left it
open. Instead of entering heroically, I
end up stumbling over the surprise of
a door slightly ajar and almost fall on
my face.

"Are you okay?" I ask Vaughn
once I regain my balance.

He glances quickly at Pater and
nods. Eloy enters the room behind
me and walks toward his brother.
They embrace each other as he
begins to quietly weep into his arms.

"You're a man now, kid. Finally

got some hair on your balls! How does it feel?" Pater asks him with a wide, shit-eating grin on his face.

I shoot him a dirty look which he chooses to ignore as he sits down on the window ledge. It wouldn't take much to rid us of this plague. I could run at him and shove him out the window and he would break his neck when he hit the pavement below, but would he die? Would it be enough to kill him?

"Oh, you've got that look on your face again, Joce. Thinking of a way to kill me, huh?" he asks with a chuckle as his grin widens, and he crosses his arms over his chest.

Pater has always said that he can read our minds, that he knows what's in our deepest thoughts, and that there are no secrets we can keep from him. Every time I've thought of ending this so far, he's proven his word on that.

"No," I reply, letting out a long suffering sigh.

"No..." his voice trails off and he raises an eyebrow. I have to fight the urge to roll my eyes so that he doesn't end up smacking them out of my head.

"No *Pater*," I amend through gritted teeth.

"You're so pretty when you're behaving," he remarks in a much softer tone. The way the words slide from his tongue, knowing the venom that he usually spews, doesn't move a goddamn thing inside of me. To be honest, I think it's meant to be a compliment, but coming from him it has about the same effect as salt in an open wound.

"Come here, baby girl," he says, holding a hand out toward me.

I don't move right away. In fact, I'm hesitant because I don't know if he plans on throwing me out of the window, like I did him.

"I'm not gonna hurt you, Jocelyn. Come here," he says again, his tone hardening slightly. I shoot a quick glance at Vaughn and Eloy before I make my way toward him.

I take his hand and allow him to intertwine his fingers with mine as he looks into my eyes. There's almost a soft calmness to them, like he wants me to learn to trust him. Like he hasn't spent the entire time here trying to destroy the three of us. Like he's worth so much more than just being feared.

"Hi," he whispers softly. I'm afraid for the boys and myself, because I've never seen this almost human side of Pater before. He seems more like a man now than someone consumed with being a completely jaded and sick moth-erfucker.

But what honestly worries me the most is that the way he holds my gaze and gently strokes the top of my hands with his thumbs is causing my body to relax. My guard is going down and I find myself feeling safe for the first time since I've been here.

"Hi," I reply, almost shyly.

Look away, Joce.

I turn my eyes down from his gaze and let out a small, shuddery sigh. I don't like this feeling, not when there's so much he needs to be held accountable for. And definitely not when I still have children to protect from his insane Messiah complex.

"I wanna talk to you privately after we're done here," he says, pulling me against him and nuzzling my ear with his lips. The stubble makes me shiver slightly and I nod. I feel the smallest glimmer of hope that maybe he'll let us all go without punishment, but I know better.

He chuckles as he spins my body around, almost in a pirouette, then moves over to sit me next to him on the window.

"Eloy," he begins in his fatherly tone, "Where were you off to just now?"

"I just wanted to see how fast he

could run," I interject, wringing my hands.

"Let him answer for himself," Pater says sternly, giving me a side-long glance. I bite my lip and nod, watching the grin return to his face as he looks back at Eloy expectantly.

"I've never really been outside by myself," he replies quietly as he wipes away the last of his tears. "I just wanted to look around."

"And you encouraged that, huh? Damn," Pater asks, shaking his head slightly as he looks at me, the grin slowly starting to fade. "I expected better from you."

I've disappointed him and it cuts me deeply that he's suggested as much. I don't want to be here, I don't want to be his fucking slave, and I don't want the boys to be harmed, but to know that I've disappointed him completely decimates the little bit of hope I have left.

"Alright, well," he says, as he gets to his feet, "I'm not going to do anything to you tonight, boy. You can go back down to your room, and you can fucking stay there until I decide I want to see your face again."

Eloy lets out a sound of relief that resembles something like another strangled sob, and Pater sighs loudly.

"Stop fucking crying already!" he shouts at Eloy as he quickly makes his escape from the room.

"He's just a child," I say quietly.

"Jocelyn, I'm trying really hard right now, so shut your fucking mouth," Pater barks at me. "You - get out. I'll come talk to you later about something. You get to bear the brunt of the bullshit these two tried to pull," he says to Vaughn as he nods toward the door.

I can see the color drain from the older boy's face, but he nods and leaves, giving me one last glance over his shoulder on the way out.

As soon as Vaughn is gone, Pater walks toward the door and closes it firmly. He lingers there for a moment, his hand on the white wood, and hangs his head. I don't know what he plans on doing to me, but I have absolutely no problem throwing myself out the window.

"But you won't, because you won't leave those boys behind," he says, straightening himself up and turning to face me. He leans against the door and crosses his arms over his chest, a vacant expression in his eyes.

"How do you do that?" I asked him quietly.

"No questions. Don't do that. Don't be a bitch right now, not when I'm trying so hard to be a good man," he says, shaking his head vehemently.

"I'm sorry," I say again, for what seems the millionth time in my captivity.

"I'm going to tell you right now that when I'm done with that little shit, you're going to hate me. More than you already do. And don't tell me you don't because I can see it in your eyes. You've been plotting against me for a long time, Jocelyn, but we've still got our *List of Tasks*, don't we? We have to finish our little game before you decide to get brave enough to make a move against me."

"I'm not going to," I say, shaking my head. "I'm not! I wouldn't!"

"You won't while they're still alive. *They* give you a reason to hold back, but I don't want that anymore. I don't want a wife that doesn't know how to take what she wants. I want you to show me you're strong enough, that you're capable of this life. We can always have more kids, but I can't have another *you*."

Pater moves away from the door and walks over to where I'm still sitting. His steps are slow, deliberate, and so fucking enticing.

"Do you really want to die before I've had a chance to fill your womb?" he asks in a whisper as he places his hands on my sides. "Don't you want to know what it's gonna feel like to grow swollen with my child? Hm? Don't you want to know what it's going to feel like when I cut the little bastard out of you?"

"What?" I ask, looking up at him. I couldn't have heard him correctly. That's too sick, even for him.

"The only reason I kept those two around was to see what kind of mother you would be," he says softly, his lips curling into a smile. "And you'll be a damn fine one if I do say so myself. We just have to get rid of them, and then we can start over. Just the two of us for a while."

"Why?" I ask, my voice shaking.

"Because that's how it's always been, baby girl. Now when I go visit Vaughn later, I don't want you to cry or be upset or even think about it. I do want you to take care of another task for me, though. Can you do that for me?"

His breath is hot on my face as he rubs his lips gently against mine, before pulling back and leaning down to look into my face.

"I want you to get rid of Eloy. We don't need him anymore."

I let out a shaky breath and choke back my sob. If I do this, it'll be merciful, I know it will. If I don't, he's going to die anyway.

"Yes, Pater," I agree in a shaky whisper.

CHAPTER EIGHT

He looks so peaceful as he sleeps; like a cherub, ignorant of the dangerous plot that's been laid out behind his back. He doesn't know that his life is meant to come to an end soon, and I won't wake him to tell him either.

I gently lay a hand on his leg and his body shivers, but he doesn't wake up. It's a natural reaction to being touched in this godforsaken place. You can wince, you can shiver, you can whimper, and you can cry, but you can never say no.

It's been a couple of hours since

I've entered the boy's room, and this is the first time I've actually touched him since being here. I've only just sat on the edge of his bed, watching his chest rise with each breath he takes in, and lower shakily with each breath he lets out.

To know that I'm here to make sure his breathing comes to an end is more of a psychological pain than anything else, but that's always been the main point of any game Pater decides to play.

"I'll either break your mind or I'll break your spirit but rest assured that I will fucking break you."

Those words have never left me. Ever since I ascended, so to speak, to the role of wife and mother, it was a credo he would repeat to me almost daily until I accepted the fact that I would never be able to leave him.

Not on my own terms, at least.

Of course, his warnings have always been sugar coated with assurances that he would never harm me more than I can bear, but what he asks of me now is just too cruel to comprehend.

I hate myself for agreeing to this, but he'll go much more peacefully at my hands than he would Pater's.

Leaning forward, I brush his hair out of his face and give him a gentle kiss on his cheek before I reach for one of the pillows on the bed. The one lying next to his head. The one that won't wake him if I try to pry it out from beneath him. The one I'll use to steal his last breath.

"Good night, my sweet boy," I whisper, a tear rolling down my cheek.

With one swift movement, I place the pillow over his head and press down as hard as I can. Since he's asleep, he's unaware what's happening, but it doesn't take long for his body to react to the lack of oxygen and his will to survive surfaces.

Eloy attempts to fight me off and

he's so valiant in his efforts that I almost stop. But I know this is what Pater wants, and it might spare Vaughn a similar fate, so I get onto the bed and straddle him, pushing down with the weight of my body to hold him in place.

"Please. Don't make this harder than it has to be. Go back to sleep, sweet boy," I whisper, pushing down harder.

His muffled cries for help are starting to fade, but he's not resigned to his fate; not yet. He continues to claw at my hands, trying his damnedest to get me to stop.

"I'm going to miss you so much," I manage to choke out as I push down even harder. "Please remember that I love you. Please."

His body is beginning to relax now, and his breaths come in three more heaping gasps before there's silence. There's no more fighting, no more hoping that this isn't really happening to him. And one less son to keep safe.

A wail escapes from deep within me. It's loud and desperate, and so heartbreaking that when I collapse against Eloy's lifeless body, I know it will take the strongest of men to pull me off him.

The door opens a moment later and I can hear the heavy footsteps of Pater as he walks toward the bed.

"Come on. Off," he says quietly as he grips my arms and pries the pillow from my hands. His small act of kindness is to leave it balanced on Eloy's face so that I don't have to see what I've done to him.

"Alright, stop crying," he says, as he uses all his strength to pull me off the boy. He struggles a bit, and I can attribute that to a mother's love for her son. For not wanting to be parted from him. Even though it was my own hands that extinguished his life, I felt I needed to still keep him safe from Pater.

"Joce. A little help here. Come on," he grunts as he gives me one hard, final yank and rips me away from the shell of Eloy.

He envelopes me in his arms and gently places a hand on the back of my head, holding me closely against his body. He's rocking slowly in an attempt to soothe the pain he's put me through, but nothing will ever be enough to wash this horrendous misdeed from my hands.

I've earned my place in Hell for this and I will gladly burn for as long as I need to purge myself of this sin.

Pater pulls me off the bed and walks us toward the door. He has to use his foot to push it all the way open because he knows that if he lets me go, I'll attempt to take my life in any way I can.

"Vaughn!" he calls out.

I begin to cry, a brand new cascade of heartache washing over me, as I try to take some comfort in knowing that my oldest child is still alive.

"Yes Pater?" his voice calls out vacantly as he approaches us.

"Take care of that," he says to him.

I dig my hands into his chest, crumpling his shirt between my fingers. A silent plea to spare Vaughn from having to see his own brother dead, but it will fall on deaf ears. It always does.

"E...Eloy?" Vaughn asks uncertainly, stepping into the room.

"He can't h...hear you," Pater mocks. "Now clean this shit up. I've gotta take care of your mother. Meet us downstairs when you're done. And if you try to run," Pater breaks off with a chuckle, "well. I'm sure you know the price now."

I pull away from his chest and look at Vaughn through eyes hazed with tears, attempting to catch his glance, but he refuses to look at me.

I don't blame him.

I'm supposed to be the one keeping them safe, and now he knows I'm just as dangerous as the man keeping us here as his prisoners. And that makes us all as equally responsible for the torments that will unfold next.

CHAPTER NINE

I've fallen into a world of half sleep. A place where Eloy is still alive, but the hand of Pater still keeps me awake as he gently strokes the side of my face, reminding me that the world I'm trying to surrender to is nothing more than a lie.

My head is resting comfortably on Pater's lap, and I can hear him whistling softly. It's just another ploy to keep me awake, but I don't want to dream. I honestly don't want to be in a place where the life I've just taken stares at me with damning eyes, asking me why I betrayed him.

It's a bit of a conundrum, really. To be in the realm of sleep where I can hold Eloy safely in my arms is more of a punishment than anything the man that helped give him life could ever dream of.

Keeping me as awake long as he possibly can helps me hold on to the thin shred of sanity I have left, but I don't know how much more I can take of these endless games. These *Tasks*, as he calls them; only two have been accomplished, and I can tell there's still so much more that needs to be done.

"Took you long enough," he says quietly.

I don't attempt to sit up to look at Vaughn. The whole point of him coming into the room and seeing me in the distress I had left myself in was part of Pater's plan. He'll never trust me again, and I can't fault him for that.

I'd take my own fucking life if it weren't for Vaughn.

"Sit down," Pater said to him, still gently stroking my hair. "I've got a little job for you."

"No," I say softly. It takes every last ounce of energy I have to push myself off Pater's lap and sit up, but when I look into his eyes, I know that any anger I incur over what I say will be worth it. "No more games. No more tasks. No more jobs. Please, just let this be the end."

"That's not how this works, and you know it, Joce. It's what you signed up for and until I say it's over, we keep going," he says, shaking his head at me. He turns his gaze back toward Vaughn as he scratches his chin. The gaze isn't returned; if anything, Vaughn looks like he's already given up and would happily collapse and die if it were allowed.

"Pater," I plead, putting a hand on his thigh. "Just me. This can all end right now with just me. I surrender to you. Let the boy go."

A grin starts to slide over his lips.

I used the words he's been trying to get out of me for so long, and I hope that by giving myself over completely to his fucking whim that it might spare the only child we have left.

"Oh yeah?" he asks, leaning back against the cough. "And all I have to do is let the boy go?"

"Yes," I say quietly.

I hope that if he agrees to this, one day Vaughn will look back on me as the mother that tried to protect him for as long as I could. Not as the mother who murdered his brother and became no better than the man he fears so much.

"I'll think about it," he says brightly, getting to his feet. "Come on, kid. Time to put you to work."

"Wait!"

I quickly get to my feet and Pater lets out a sigh before pushing me back down.

"Stay," he commands, holding up one finger. "I'm not gonna hurt him, so I need you to just calm down and stay fucking put. I'll be back."

Vaughn quietly begins to follow Pater out of the room, and even though I know it'll fall on deaf ears, I can't let this possibly be the last time I see him without saying what I feel in my heart.

"I love you, Vaughn," I call out to him urgently.

He doesn't return the sentiment. He doesn't even cast me one final glance, and even though Pater said he's not going to hurt him, I can't help but feel like this is the last time I'll ever see him again.

"Wait," Pater says to him sternly. "Your mother is talking to you; show a little respect, huh?"

Vaughn clenches his fists by his sides and turns slowly to look at me. We finally lock eyes, but the look he gives me tells me I've lost him.

"She's *not* my mother."

CHAPTER TEN

The pain of his words wounds me as deeply as what I was forced to do to Eloy, but it's because he speaks a bitter truth. An honesty that is so raw and uncommon in this house that hearing it for the first time since this entire charade started is like a blow to the heart.

I don't know how long it's been since they've left this room. Time means nothing when everything you love has collapsed around you because of your own actions. When your will is no longer your own and you're forced to survive by any means dictated to you, you do what you must.

What happens when you choose to fight against the will of Pater is far worse than what I did to Eloy, and what he's most likely doing to Vaughn. For now, I'll comply. I'll listen. I'll take every blow to my heart until it finally gives out, and because of my choices, I'll survive.

"Hey, you alright?"

A strong hand rests gently on my shoulder and I shudder. Not out of revulsion, but the need to feel his touch comforting me. Pater may be an evil man when it comes to many things, myself included, but he always attempts to make sure I'm okay.

"I'll be fine," I whisper as a tear rolls down my cheek.

He crouches down and uses his hand to gently lift my face up. He's searching my eyes, looking for some sign of deception, but he'll find none.

I *will* be fine.

I always am.

"Come on. You can stay in my bed tonight," he says, gently pulling me off the ground.

"I don't..." *want to,* I finish to myself. While I appreciate his comforting hands on me, that's all I want. I don't want to feel him roughly moving inside of me until he's satisfied himself with no regard for how much it hurts me.

"I'm not looking for anything tonight, Joce. Especially not any arguments," he replies tiredly. "I just want you to have somewhere comfortable to sleep."

I let him get me to my feet, but he can tell I have no intention of following him.

"Alright, you've got two choices," he says, rubbing his stubble irritably. "You can sleep in my bed, or I can throw you back into that hole. Ladies' choice."

Normally the answer would be

simple and instantaneous, but there's nothing normal about this anymore. Eloy is dead. Vaughn is... I don't even know where the hell Vaughn is. And the man that took him from me doesn't seem like he's going to talk about it, either.

My heart is telling me to accept the oubliette. After all, I still owe him a day in the darkness and solitude, but my mind is telling me to stay in his bed. I won't be of any use to Vaughn if I'm tired and hungry and being in the house will afford me the chance to rest and eat when Pater falls asleep.

"I have a condition," I say, as I wipe away tears. "Will you meet it?"

Pater looks at me through narrowed eyes, but nods in acceptance. Since this is his home and we abide by his rules, he's not bound to any promise he makes. I know it just as much as he does, but I can only hope he'll allow me this small token of kindness.

"I want to know what you've done with Vaughn," I reply, crossing my arms over my chest and meeting his narrowed eyes with a stubborn stare.

A slow, malicious grin spreads across his handsome face and I can feel myself starting to waiver in the mock confidence I've presented.

"I dumped him," he says, chuckling. "If he doesn't have respect for his mother, he definitely doesn't have any for his father. Can't keep a little shit like that around."

In an odd moment of clarity, I'm surprised that I feel nothing. No more sorrow, no more hope, no more hatred toward Pater. And what I feel least of all as his words ring through my mind is my soul.

It's gone now.

All of it.

By taking both the boys from me, he's taken everything. It's just me and Pater now, and by his assuming that he's relieved me of the duties of

being a mother, he's given me something else I haven't felt in years.

The will to fight.

CHAPTER ELEVEN

Pater has his arm wrapped tightly enough around me that I can't leave the bed without him knowing, but loose enough that I'm free to move around until I'm comfortable.

"Hey, Joce?" he asks, punctuating his question with a wide yawn.

"Yes Pater?" I ask tiredly.

I'm holding his arm tightly, almost as though I'm trying to pull something good out of the cesspool that he's become, but I know it's all in vain.

"When I said I dumped Vaughn? You didn't ask where."

"It's not my place to question you, Pater," I reply quietly.

He chuckles as he nuzzles up closer to me. "I'm glad you chose to come with me. I didn't want to put you in the oubliette. It would have made things too crowded."

"What?" I ask in confusion.

"And I'm not exactly sure he's alive, anyway. I did give him one hell of a push, after all," he admits sleepily.

It's another mind game; a trick. If I believe that Vaughn is alive, he knows I won't resist him, but if I believe he's dead, I'll gladly go to my death and take Pater with me.

"What's a girl to do?" he asks in a sing-song voice. He chuckles as he begins to run his fingers up and down my arm. The slight tingling sensation, the shock-wave his touch sends throughout my body, makes me both sick and almost happy.

Almost.

"I guess we'll just have to wait and see," I reply as evenly as I can. It takes more bravery than I've ever mustered before to lay a challenge so boldly at his feet, and another chuckle is his response. He's accepted I'll do what I must in order to end this entire fucking charade, and I know he won't make it easy.

"Tomorrow, baby girl. We'll worry about all of this tomorrow," he says, sliding his arm around my waist and pulling me closer to him still.

"And the day after that?" I ask, turning to face him.

"Will there be another day?" he inquires, looking into my eyes.

"You're leaving it up to me?" I ask in surprise.

A smile spreads across his full lips. He turns himself onto his back and folds an arm underneath his head. Taking a deep breath and letting it out, he keeps his eyes trained on the ceiling and I can tell he is very carefully picking his next words.

"Honestly? No. I prefer if you would just go along and say there will be another day after tomorrow, and a day after that. I know this hasn't been easy for you, but at some point, I'm really gonna need you to just *try*. Think you can do that for me?"

The truth is that I *have* been trying. I've done everything Pater has asked of me, and he still wants more. There's no satisfying a man of his appetites, regardless of what they are, and my only reasons for even caring are either dead or dying.

And here I am lying in his bed like a whore, ready to please the man who bought her affections for the night.

"Pater?" I ask, as I sit up in the bed and pull my knees up to my chest.

"Yes, Jocelyn?"

"Can I speak freely?"

"Yes."

I take a deep breath and wrap my arms around my knees, resting my face against them so I can look at him. His reactions never lie; he may have a serpent's tongue, but his face will always betray him and tell me the truth.

"Why are you doing this? Wouldn't it be so much easier to kill me too?" I ask quietly.

He closes his eyes for a moment and when he opens them, I can almost swear I see tears forming. But Pater doesn't cry; he's the man of this house, and the only emotions he's ever shown us are the ones he chooses. Crying is for the weak, according to him, and Pater is far from weak.

"Because the three of you have always been my favorites," he replies irritably. "Now go the fuck to sleep or I'm dumping you in the fucking ground with Vaughn."

His attempt at a threat actually

makes me laugh. To think I would fear death at this point when I would gladly decompose by my son's side is laughable to me.

"Don't bother. I'll throw myself in the fucking pit," I say, getting off the bed and walking toward the door.

"Hey. HEY!" he bellows as soon as I open it.

I turn and give him a sharp glare, watching his face go from anger to amusement in a matter of seconds. He pats the empty side of the bed next to him where I was sitting not moments before, and I sigh.

A part of me wants to see tomorrow and the day after, but the heroine in me wants to see this come to an end.

"You coming? Or do I have to fetch you?" he asks, tilting his head to the side, the grin widening over his face.

It's maddening.

This entire fucking thing is

maddening because I do love him in a way, but I loathe him just the same.

One more night.

One more day.

When I wake up in the morning, I'll have decided if it's worth seeing the day after.

CHAPTER TWELVE

I wake up with a terrible headache and the weight of the world on top of me. It's astounding to me that I was able to sleep at all, but now I'm awake I find myself in a terrible situation.

Pater's face is hovering inches from mine, and his breathing is slightly labored. It's not the weight of the world I feel lying on top of me, it's the weight of the man that holds me here against my will. He's pushing his cock inside me, slowly, deliberately; in a way that only Pater can. He wanted me to wake up to find him on top of me. He wanted me to feel every thrust he's been lovingly pushing into me while I slept.

He wanted me to experience everything he promised me he didn't want the night before, and it's because he wants me to understand that he's the one who will decide if tomorrow comes or not.

"You're so pretty when you sleep," he whispers, brushing his lips against mine.

I hate my body for reacting to this. I didn't consent to this. I didn't want to wake up to him fucking me, but I did consent to be in his bed, so I shouldn't have expected anything less.

"Pater's almost done, baby girl," he says softly, as his breathing becomes even more labored.

He gently places his forehead against mine as I lie beneath him, pinned to the bed and waiting for him to fill me with his seed. It's what he wants most of all. He wants me to become a mother – he always has – I've just been able to convince him otherwise, since we still had Vaughn and Eloy.

It takes no more than three thrusts before I feel the warmth of him spilling into me. He lets out a loud moan as he finishes and lets his body fall on mine, his head lying on my shoulder.

"You're going to make such an amazing mother again someday. You did such a wonderful job with those two little bastards," he says gently.

"Thank you, Pater," I say quietly, fighting tears that are dangerously close to spilling over.

I place my hands on his shoulders and attempt to give him a gentle shove, but he's still hard and still inside me, showing no signs of moving.

"Not yet, Joce. Let's just lay here like this a little while longer," he says happily, turning his head up toward me and nuzzling my neck with his lips.

I can't help but wonder if this is what love is like. To have someone who would do anything to keep you, no matter the cost, with no care of what the outside world would think.

I finally feel him become flaccid and he pulls himself out of me, turning his back to me as he gets comfortable on the bed.

Maybe it's not love, after all.

"When did you start to hate me?" he asks quietly. "And don't lie to me, please."

The question takes me by surprise, because I was always so damn sure he never cared what I thought of him. His demand for the truth tells me he'll do his mind reading trick that still fascinates me.

"When you made me your wife," I reply bluntly.

Pater sighs loudly and rolls onto his back. "Would you have preferred that I just killed you instead?"

"Yes," I admit softly.

"Sorry to disappoint you," he spits back bitterly. He sits up and runs his hands over his face, then sighs as he glances at me. "You have to understand something. I've always loved you the most. That day that I cut you from your worthless mother was the happiest day of my life. You stopped crying as soon as I held you against me, and the way you looked at me..." Pater's words trail off for a moment as he shakes his head, "I knew right then and there that we would be something great someday."

"If I knew that this is what my life was going to become, along with Vaughn and Eloy's, I should have just drawn the blades across our throats when you took us out of Mama," I spit back.

His desperate attempt at trying to become some kind of human right before my eyes are falling on deaf ears. I've had enough of these fucking games, and with as much as I want it to be over, I want my pound of flesh first. The only way to get that from him is to antagonize him to the point of no return.

"'Mama'," he repeats in a mocking tone. "She was worthless. The only thing that bitch was good for was giving me three kids, and then, once Eloy was born, I was done with her. She died the way she came into this world: screaming and covered in blood."

I attempt to push myself off the bed, but he grips me by my arm and pulls me right back next to him.

"It doesn't have to be this way with us, Jocelyn. Ever since I put you in your mother's womb, I knew you would take her place. Like she had taken the place of the wife before her. I think we work, don't you? You're a pain in the ass and I know how to handle you accordingly. I like these games and being inside you is the most amazing thing I've ever felt in my life. Fuck society and their rules; we're meant to be together," he says with his damn grin sitting on his ruggedly handsome face.

The same face that was vaguely reflected in Vaughn, and almost an exact match to Eloy's. The eyes I'm looking into are passed down through blood, and that smile is something I used to wear before all this started. But I have to remind myself that this hasn't been the face of my father for a long time; it's always been the face of the man who destroys everything he can't control and uses people until he gets bored with them.

"How much longer is this going to drag on, Pater? How much longer am I stuck here being your wife?" I ask him irritably.

"Until you have my baby, of course," he replies as his grin widens. "Then we'll see what fate has in store for you."

That's been his plan this entire time. That's been his motive in every wife he's taken.

Isolate the body.

Break the soul.

Break the spirit.

Fill them with his child and if the child is up to his standards, kill her and replace her with the next one.

CHAPTER THIRTEEN

Pater is sitting at the dining room table, reading his newspaper, and occasionally sipping on his coffee. He's invited me to sit with him, but so far the offer of food has not been made, and I'm close to snatching that fucking paper from his hands and eating it.

I don't know when the last time is that I ate. It must have been a few days ago, when one of the boys dropped some scraps into the darkness, and with as unbelievable as it may seem, that's usually enough to hold me over for a little while.

I have to check the oubliette.

Clearing my throat, I begin to drum my fingers along the tabletop. It's a small enough distraction that he peers at me over the top of his newspaper, before he reaches over and puts his hand on mine to stop me.

"What's up?" he asks curiously.

"I'm more worried about what's down," I reply tiredly.

"What?"

A rare look of confusion crosses his face, and I sigh as I slide my hand away from underneath his. I glance out the window behind him, and don what I hope is a meaningful look, but if he understands what I want, he's choosing to ignore it.

"Well?" he asks, shaking out his newspaper. He licks his thumb as he flips the page and keeps his eyes trained on me expectantly.

"I'm hungry," I admit quietly. It's not exactly a lie, but it's not the entire truth. I *am* hungry; however,

I'm more concerned with taking my scraps to Vaughn.

If he's still alive.

"You can eat," he says with a nod as he turns his eyes back to his article. I almost faint with relief because he's never given us food so easily. I think it has to be because he's already attempting to make me pregnant, so it makes him slightly kinder.

I know better, though. I know that trusting a man like Pater, no matter what the circumstance, is a more dangerous game than anything he could possibly dream up.

"Thank you," I reply softly.

I get to my feet and walk toward the counter where there is still one steak left on a greasy plate. There's a spoonful of home fries and one strip of bacon, too. I quickly pile it onto a clean plate and, as I'm placing it into the microwave for a quick reheat, I hear Pater slide his chair back.

In a matter of a few steps, he's standing next to me, washing his hands in the sink, and I can feel myself start to tremble again. I know he feels my fear when he gives me a sidelong glance and smirks. He doesn't say anything, though. He dries his hands off on a dishtowel, pulls the drawer open next to me, and fishes out a fork. Once the microwave dings, he opens the door, pulls out the plate and takes it back to the table.

I'm two seconds away from throwing the mother of all tantrums, when I see that he's set the fork and plate where I had been sitting. As he makes his way back to his seat and newspaper, he clears his throat and continues to read.

"Make sure you eat every last thing on that plate, baby girl. I know you kids had some kind of system with whatever you swore you just couldn't eat, but don't forget you're the only kid now."

He's lying.

I know he's lying because I can

still feel something in my heart that's only lived there since I was put in charge of Eloy and Vaughn.

"Hey, don't you have a birthday coming up soon?" he asks conversationally.

"Yes."

"Any idea what you'll be wanting?"

"I haven't thought about it," I say, finally taking a bite of the steak. My stomach growls loudly and Pater chuckles but makes no further mention of the disruptive sound.

"Well, how long do we have until it's time to celebrate, Joce?" he asks, setting his paper down and smoothing out the pages with his hands.

With another sigh and shrug, I take a second bite of the steak. It doesn't matter how long I feel we have, or how long it will actually be until my birthday. The only thing that matters is when Pater will be ready to dedicate a moment to the day. It doesn't hold any special meaning to me anymore, my birthday. If anything, it's a day I've come to loathe. I wasn't born into normal surroundings.

I was born into a world where evil existed long before I was conceived, and where innocence goes to die.

"How old are you these days, Jocelyn?" Pater asks, resting his chin in the palm of his hand. He glances up at me when I don't answer him right away, and I'm terrified he's caught me scraping food off the plate into my lap.

"I'll be twenty, I think," I reply, as I grab the fork and slice another piece off the steak. I'm not sure what it was exactly that I managed to scoop off the plate, but I hadn't expected him to ask me something so personal. It's not like Pater to give a shit, and he should know the answer to that question anyway.

"Huh," he says indifferently.

"That's about the same age your mother was when she had Vaughn. Eh, I might have to sit through more boys again."

"Pater?" I ask carefully. Now he's mentioned Mama, I have a few questions of my own. "May I ask you something?"

He looks at me for a moment as he considers my request. He sucks his teeth before turning his eyes back down to the newspaper.

"Sure, kid."

"If I'm the oldest, why *did* you keep getting Mama pregnant?"

Pater lets out a sigh as he closes his newspaper and runs a hand over his face. The good thing is that he doesn't look angry at my question; he actually looks thoughtful.

"Nothing in the world is more beautiful than seeing the woman you love swollen with your child. Your mother was definitely a good looking gal, and even though I had already fallen in love with you by that point,

I wanted to be able to get a couple of more years out of her. I knew I would have to wait a long time before I could make you my wife, and she knew it too, so she did everything she could to keep me satisfied until I was bored with her. There's only so many times you can keep fucking the same hole before it becomes redundant, you know?"

He's looking at me knowingly, and I know I've still got at least one seed's worth of growing to do before he decides if he's going to kill me or keep me.

"Don't worry about that shit right now, though. I just told you I've been in love with you for your entire life. I have no intentions of getting rid of you. I think grooming the next bride days are done. It'll be you and me and our children until we both die," he says, with that damn wide grin spreading across his face.

I sit back and fold my arms over my chest, taking him in. Years mean nothing to me because I stopped counting them when I turned fifteen. That's when he took me as his wife and I lost the title of daughter, but I'm becoming more and more curious the older I get, and I have one more question for him.

"Pater?" I ask softly.

"Yes, baby girl?" he asks, still grinning.

"How old are you?"

He chuckles and hangs his head for a moment, before glancing back up at me. His grin has faded into a simple smile, and he doesn't answer me right away.

"Well, that depends, I guess," he replies mischievously.

I raise an eyebrow but say nothing. I don't want to continue to ask him questions and anger him instead of just getting a simple answer.

"Will it make you love me any less? Assuming that you do love me, that is," he says with a smirk.

I *do* love Pater. I will never deny

that, but I don't love him in the manner that he wants me to. I love him as a father who lost his way long before I was born and needs saving, even though I know he doesn't want to be saved.

"No," I say softly.

He grins, gets up from his chair, and walks around the table toward me. Pater puts an arm around my shoulder and kisses the top of my head gently.

"Good girl. I knew you'd always love me as much as I love you," he says gently. "You about done with that?"

Before I have a chance to answer, or save any more food for Vaughn, he takes the plate from the table and dumps the remnants into the trash can. I use his distracted moments to shove the bit of food I've managed to scavenge into the bottom of my shirt and roll it up just enough to make sure it can't fall out.

"You can go out and throw him

what you've saved," he says with a tired sigh. "If he's still alive, I'm sure he'll appreciate it."

And with that, he walks out of the kitchen leaving me with one last unanswered question, and the moment I need to go save Vaughn.

CHAPTER FOURTEEN

He's going to kill me.

I know he is because that's the end game. No matter what he says, no matter how much he professes his love for me, I know it's the only thing that can come of this.

I'll never be the wife he wants me to be, and I'll never be more than a scared child praying for the safety of the children forced underneath her rule, instead of being by her side as it should have been in a normal world.

To survive much longer than I know I'm meant to, I'll have to be more careful. He knows too much, sees more than I think he does, and he'll stop me when he feels I'm getting ready to strike.

He'll be the end of me. He'll send me to the afterlife with a smile on his face once he has another child to hold in his arms, but I will take a part of his soul with me.

I won't think about it now. I still have Vaughn to worry about, and I don't think he knows that Eloy is still alive somewhere in the woods. That's where Vaughn would have taken him because that's their safe place away from this hell we have to endure.

I can see the top of the oubliette from here and I stop walking, taking a deep breath. I have to prepare for the worst, because if I hope for the best and it's not there, it'll crush me completely.

I've managed to save one son so far by putting on one hell of a show, and I know I won't be able to handle not saving the second.

Please, I pray silently as I kneel down by the broken door that sits on top. I close my eyes for a moment, trying to find the courage to do what I know has to be done, to calm my nerves and steel myself against what I hope I don't see before I finally pull the door open.

It's dark in the oubliette, but that's the point. To be encased below the ground in the darkness, with only the occasional chirping of birds, or the crickets at night; the punishment always fits the crime, and if Pater has banished you to the underground dungeon, the transgression must have been severe.

It's my second home because I defy him so frequently to protect Vaughn and Eloy, but I don't mind it as much as he thinks I do. From what I know so far, he hasn't laid his hands upon them in any form of sexual deviance, and because of that, when I'm in the dark, I sleep more soundly than I do in his bed.

It's the days leading up to my freedom that always make me anxious. That's when I lose the most sleep because I have to face my children and hope they're still safe from having to feel his touch.

A pocket of air was enough to save Eloy; maybe the will to survive the fall will have been enough to save Vaughn.

I let out my breath in a rush of quick air as I lean over the side. I can't see him from the top of the pit, which means he's huddled in a corner, or dead where he's fallen.

"Vaughn?" I call down quietly, my voice cracking. I take a deep breath, clear my throat, and try again. "Vaughn? It's me; Jocelyn."

Silence greets me in return. I blink furiously to keep tears from falling and call out his name again.

"Vaughn?"

I feel like the world is slowly starting to crush me into the ground when I still receive no answer, and just as I'm ready to accept that he's gone, I can almost swear that I hear a slight shifting sound at the bottom of the pit.

"I have food!" I call back down as I unroll the bottom of my shirt and drop it into the pit. The sound I heard could very well be the rats that make the inside of the walls their home, but I'm too stubborn to give up all my hope until I know for sure.

My entire problem is that I'm blinded by the one thing I refuse to let go of. Hope that Vaughn is still alive. Hope that Eloy is safe, wherever he is. Hope that Pater will see the madness in this entire scheme and let us go.

My own worst enemy is the only fucking thing I keep hanging on to. If I learn to let go, I know things will become clearer; this will all end the way it's meant to, and not how Pater wants it to.

There are no further sounds coming from the darkness below, and there's no sign of movement. If Vaughn is still alive down there, he doesn't trust me enough to let me know.

I can't blame him.

He walked into a nightmare, thinking that his younger brother was dead at my hands, but even when he realized he wasn't, he couldn't find it in himself to forgive me for tricking him into thinking otherwise.

I'm okay with it.

I have to be.

If he doesn't trust me, it will only make his will stronger, and maybe it's him and not me who will be the one to end all this.

"Find what you were looking for?"

I jump in complete shock at hearing Pater's voice coming from above me, almost losing ground and falling into the pit, but he's faster and much stronger than me, and manages to pull me back before it happens.

He gets me to my feet, giving me an unbelievably harsh glare, prompting only a nod in return. I won't attempt to mimic the look he's giving me. He's won this round and he knows it, because if he thought otherwise, he would be smiling at me instead of sneering.

"Why are you always so content to defy me?" he asks in a low, even tone.

"What? You told me I could--"

Pater smacks me so violently that I fall back onto the ground and come dangerously close to plummeting into the darkness. He gets on his knees in front of me and grips me tightly by the arms. He makes no move to pull me away from the abysmal opening, instead leaning my body further into it.

"Don't play dumb, Jocelyn. And drop the fucking innocent act. I thought we actually understood each other at this point, but you still seem to be full of games, and we can't have that," he says, as he tips me a little further back.

My hands immediately clench his wrists. If he throws me in, I'm going to make damn sure he comes with me. Ending this now would be premature, but why does he deserve to breathe another breath when those of us that were chosen for this are considered so easily disposable?

I take a deep breath and clench my jaw tightly. The pressure of being bent in such an unnatural manner is starting to hurt me, but I refuse to let go of his wrists. I'm not as strong as Pater, and I'm not as fast as him, but I hold an equal amount of determination as him, if not more.

"I think we need to go back to the beginning here, Jocelyn. I think we need to go back to the very first Task I gave you, and complete it together," he says meaningfully.

I close my eyes tightly and do my best not to cry. He knows; of course he knows. I was stupid enough to think about how I saved Eloy, and Pater picked it out of my brain.

"Where is he?" he asks, pulling me back toward him. I'm inches from his face now. I know because I can feel his breath on my face, as well as the rage radiating from his body. It's equally terrifying and intoxicating.

"I don't know," I reply truthfully.

"Do you really want it to end like this?" he asks me angrily, giving me one, hard shake. "We have plans, Jocelyn, and you're willing to throw it all away on some bastards that aren't worth more than dog shit on the bottom of a shoe? Give me one good reason I shouldn't drop you into this fucking hole."

I take a deep breath and open my eyes. Pater's face is twisted in hideous rage and genuine confusion, and for the slightest of moments I feel bad for betraying him.

My heart aches slightly when I'm confronted by the complete and utter hurt on the face of my own personal devil, knowing now that he's been betrayed.

"Because I'm the only hope you have for a new family," I respond quietly.

He lets out a guffaw, and his hands begin to shake. He knows it's the truth, and that's why I can now openly go against his will. He's laid his cards bare on the table and foolishly told me he needs me, allowing me to use it to my full advantage.

In the rare moment Pater tried to be nothing more than a man in love, he sealed his own fate. He showed me that I'm his weakness, and that he needs me now more than I need him.

Even though the realization hits in this moment, holding me on the brink of life and death, I don't plan on using it to my advantage. Not until I can get Vaughn out of the darkness and make sure that he and Eloy can find their own safety far away from this place.

CHAPTER FIFTEEN

The soles of my feet are scraped raw
from walking the property barefoot,
since I've agreed to go into the woods
with Pater and try to locate the
young boy. I figure it's a small price
to pay. He says if we find Eloy and
finish what I should have done
together, he'll assist me with getting
Vaughn out of the oubliette.

"I really think we should have
Vaughn with us right now," I grum-
ble. "I don't know where he hid Eloy.
I don't know if he's even still *here*."

Pater tightens his grip on my arm

and shakes his head. "He's still here. Know how I know? Because you don't want to help look for him. You want to pawn this off on Vaughn, and you hoped I would fall for it. I'm not as stupid as you'd like to think I am, Jocelyn. Vaughn earned his time in the hole. Eloy earned his punishment. And you're going to be a good little wife and follow through on what you've promised me."

Pater stops walking abruptly and glances down at me with a devious smirk on his face and cruel intentions in his eyes.

"Tell you what," he says, licking his lips and pulling me toward him. "You help me take care of this, make it all the way it should be again, and I'll take you to see your precious Mama."

I stare at Pater with wide eyes and the most doubt and confusion I've ever felt in my life. How can he take me to see her when he's already told me she's dead?

It has to be where she's buried. That's the only thing that would make sense with a promise like that, isn't it?

"How far in do you think he is?" Pater asks, running his hand down the length of my arm and intertwining his fingers with mine.

I shake my head. I don't know; I really don't. I only assume, as he does, that this is where Eloy would be because it's his favorite place to go when he's allowed outside. Of course, after the debacle with Laura, I honestly doubt that he would want to wallow in whatever memories his mind was forced to create.

"Alright, then you can go first," he says, letting go of my hand and pushing me in front of him. It's not that he's afraid; nothing scares Pater. His intention is that if there is a boy to be found and I'm seen before him, then the confidence would be there to make himself known.

It's a fucking trap, and I'm the

bait. What will happen if Eloy steps forward unknowingly? Will Pater end him right then and there, or will he leave the task up to me again? He'll watch, I know he will, and he'll make sure that this time it's done to completion, and the blood I've tried so quietly to save will flow freely over my hands.

"May I have a moment first?" I plead, turning to face him. My hands automatically go to his chest, the safest place I knew as a child, and I can see it still has an effect on him by the rapid way he blinks.

"Only a moment," he agrees with a sharp nod.

I pull away from him and immediately begin to push through the low hanging tree branches and over-grown brush. Pater won't give me more time than he feels is warranted, and I haven't even earned these precious moments he's given me.

He should have just thrown me

back into the darkness. If he had thrown me back in after Laura was disposed of, this wouldn't be happening. This is all my fault.

A sob escapes me as I reach the clearing. There's a rather large circle of trees that span a patch of dirt in the woods. A large stone sits in the center of it, with smaller rocks scattered about, almost like a tiny village of sorts.

In the large stone, there's a makeshift chair; a throne. It was there before me, and it'll be there after me because I do not believe him when he tells me I'm the last. It was the chair I sat in after he bound us together as husband and wife. He said the chair held special meaning, that it would help us survive any obstacle set before us, and yet I can't help but find only lies in a truth only he believes.

In that stone chair, there's now a body, slumped over and bleeding. I can't tell if there's still life inside it or not. It's hard to even tell if it's human from where I am, and since I don't have time to waste, I run over and stop just short of it.

It's Eloy.

Bloodied, bruised, damn near mangled, with a pile of rocks sitting around him. He's not alive; he can't be. Vaughn did the one thing I couldn't do. He saved his brother from a life of anguish, misuse, and deviance.

By stoning him to death.

Placing him in the chair afterwards was symbolic. It was his way of saying that the bond between Pater and I isn't real, that I could have saved all of us had I only managed to muster up the courage he was forced to have.

Did he tell his brother he loved him before he killed him? Did he tell his brother that even though this isn't how life is supposed to be, I tried my best and loved him too? Did he tell his brother that, no matter how long it takes, we'll rid the world of Pater and his evil ways? Did he tell his brother that he'll never have to see either of us again in the afterlife?

Did his brother believe him if he did?

Vaughn was the only one he could trust, and since I don't see any evidence that he was bound to the carved chair, I know he willingly gave up his life so that Vaughn wouldn't suffer if Pater found him alive.

He sacrificed himself to save his brother and give Pater one less person to deal with. He saved himself by welcoming death, and I stand here a coward, unwilling to go down as easily because I'm wracked with thoughts of vengeance.

But the first Task is done to completion, as Pater would have seen it, and as I turn to walk away from Eloy's lifeless corpse, I feel rage in the empty spot of my heart that once held unconditional love for him.

My son is dead for the second time, because I wasn't strong enough to put an end to the monster that holds us here.

CHAPTER SIXTEEN

"Damn."

Pater has finally made it into the clearing and is shaking his head in what looks like appreciation.

"Rocks, huh?" he asks, crouching down in front of Eloy's torn body. "I wonder which one of them chose that. Must have hurt like hell."

"Eloy," I say softly, a single tear slowly trickling down my cheek. "He always liked looking at nature. It's only fitting that he chose it as his end."

"Guess I really should've got to know him. I always feel so damn bad when you tell me things about these kids that I didn't know," he says, reaching up and pushing his face back. I can see the cuts and scrapes on Eloy's face now. His eyes are still open, but vacant. They're looking into a void that neither of us can see, one we should have gone to in his place.

"What's your next Task?" I ask Pater. He glances up at me curiously as he lets the boy's chin fall back onto his chest and stands back up. I wait patiently as he crosses his arms over his chest and looks up at the trees.

"They weren't really tasks, Joce. They were tests of your loyalty to me, and as much as I hate to say it, you failed, baby girl."

"So kill me, and fucking get it over with," I shout in desperation, shoving him as hard as I can.

Pater rolls his eyes and reaches for my arms as I try to shove him again, forcing them to fold over my chest.

"If I kill you, we can't have forever. I promised you forever, and I plan on keeping that promise," he says in a soft voice.

"You promised Mama forever. And the one before her the same thing, and the one before *her*. What makes me so fucking special that you have to keep doing this to me? Haven't you destroyed me enough?" I scream at him as I try to rip my arms away from his vice grip.

Pater gives me one firm shake to stop my hysterics, before wrapping his arms tightly around me and holding me close to him. He looks deeply into my eyes, almost soulfully, and I can tell that whatever words he chooses to speak next are of some meaning to him. Whether *I'll* find any meaning in them is of no consequence. Anything I could have ever felt for this monster is as dead as the boy listening to us with hollow ears.

"If you want me to answer you honestly, I'm gonna need you to calm the fuck down and listen," he says sternly. "If you insist on flailing around like a fucking lunatic, I'll just tell you what you want to hear and make you believe it. It's up to you."

With that, he releases me and steps back, crossing his arms over his chest and waiting for me to make my choice. Pater is a patient monster, and he's used to always getting his way. This time will be no different, I decide, as I push my hair back from my face and nod in agreement.

Pater clears his throat and runs a hand over his chin. There seems to be more gray hair than black now, and his eyes look so tired that I almost feel bad for him. He's been through a lot, not as much as the three...two of us have, but he seems to be feeling the weight of his decisions finally starting to press down against whatever humanity he tries to hide deep inside of him.

"Alright. Yes, there were others before your mother, but she was the first one that actually gave me kids. The others before her tried but could never conceive. Either that, or they aborted and never told me - I don't know. Since you were my first born, you held so much more meaning to me than anything else in the world. You're a symbol that I actually did something right for once in my life, and I tried not to fuck things up, Jocelyn; you have to believe that. I *tried*." He takes a deep breath for a moment and closes his eyes tightly before opening them again and looking back into mine. "Did I mean for all of this to happen? Yeah; I honestly did, but not like this. I wanted those boys to stay alive even though I didn't have any fucking use for them, because I could see that they made you happy. And once I realized that you could make *me* happy in every way a man could feel, I got rid of your mother. She would have just gotten in the way and tried to stop us from being together. Don't you wanna be with me, Joce? After everything we've been through?"

The tone of his voice is bordering on pleading, but he doesn't change his demeanor to match, and it leaves me confused.

Would I have ever thought this way of living was okay? At one point, I didn't know any better. I thought this was how a father loved his children, because when he plucked my innocence from a garden I've long since burned to the ground, I did love him. In every way he wanted me to, I loved him.

The older I became and the more he pushed Vaughn and Eloy away, the endless nights spent in the oubliette, and the constant having to stay awake to keep the boys safe wore down every thread I was hanging onto that made me believe, once upon a time, that Pater was worthy of my love.

"We've been through nothing together," I begin quietly. "You forced this life on me. On Eloy. On Vaughn. We didn't have a choice in any of this, and because your love is so weak that you chose only one of us to care for instead of all of us, I can't say that I want anything with you, much less forever."

He puts his hands on his hips and looks away. I can see it now, the monster inside of him coming to the surface, but I don't stop. After all, he offered me honesty, and I feel it's only fair to offer him honesty in return.

"This *will* come to an end someday soon, and one of us won't survive. The only question left to answer between us is who."

"Don't do that. Don't make idle fucking threats when you know I can snap your neck any time I want to," he warns, shaking his head vehemently.

"But you won't. You want another child, and I refuse to give you one, knowing what you're going to put it through," I spit back stubbornly. "Now, if you'll excuse me, I have to go back to that fucking hell in the ground you're so keen on keeping us in and retrieve Vaughn. Dead or alive, he deserves to be with Eloy, and that's exactly where I'm going to put him."

As I spin on my heel with fire in my veins, I can hear Pater call my name out, but I don't stop or turn toward him.

He's had too many chances to make this right again, and he's always chosen the path that best suited his needs. His disregard for us, the death of Eloy, the possibility of finding Vaughn dead in the pit will be his downfall. His reckoning is coming, and I will be the hand that delivers it, so help me God.

CHAPTER SEVENTEEN

I don't go directly to the oubliette. Instead, I walk back into the house, making my way down the entire length until I reach the front door.

A-ha! It's still there.

I gather up the rope ladder that Vaughn had used to rescue me and open the front door. I can hear Pater calling my name as he makes his way toward me. He sounds damn angry at being disregarded, but it's time he knows what that feels like for once.

Pater's taller and much faster than me, so I know he'll catch up to me if I don't quicken my steps. I throw the rope over my shoulder and begin to jog toward my destination. If he won't tell me what's really happened to Vaughn, I'll climb down into the abyss and find out myself. Besides, seeing it with my own eyes will serve my intentions much better than hearing a story venomously packed with sweetened lies.

"JOCELYN!"

Pater's booming voice as he exits the front of the house almost stops me, but I need to know what happened to Vaughn, and I need to know now.

I break into a run. As fast as my legs will carry me, I fucking run. I reach the top of the dungeon in no time and flip the door open. I quickly wrap a large part of the rope ladder around the cylindrical stone and pray that it holds as I toss the rest of the ladder over the side. I give it one hard tug and I'm over the side, descending into the darkness.

"Goddamn it!" Pater yells angrily.

I glance up momentarily to see him leaning down into the oubliette, attempting to reach for me, but I'm already too far down for him to snatch me back up.

"Fucking kids," he shouts, slapping his hand against the door before he disappears from sight.

Good.

He's angry and he knows he can't reach me, because there's no way in hell he'll crawl in here to retrieve me.

Pater is afraid of the things he can't control, and the darkness is *my* home, not his.

There's not a lot of room to move down at the bottom, but what little space there is I know like the back of my hand.

"Vaughn?" I call out as I come closer to the bottom.

Please be okay, I will desperately.

I'm nothing like Pater; I can't think of things and make them happen. I can't read minds, and I can't take control of people's lives, but what I can do that he can't or won't do is help those who need it the most.

I don't deserve help, because I should have been able to save us from this, but I was too blinded by his deceptions for so long that I welcomed everything he did to us.

I don't know if I'll ever be able to leave Pater. My world would crumble without him, and I know it, but if I can just save *one* of these boys, then I'll be okay with being left behind.

The ladder is too short to get me all the way to the bottom, since I wrapped a good portion of it around the opening, so I hop down the last couple of feet and hope that if Vaughn is alive, he'll either be capable of pulling himself up, or give me enough help to get us both out of here.

"Vaughn?" I ask into the darkness. I rub my hands together before wiping them on my thighs and narrow my eyes.

I'm not a nocturnal animal, but it's easy for my eyes to adjust to the darkness they know so well, and from what I can tell, he's not standing if he's down here. Dropping to my knees, I begin to crawl in a small circle, following the pattern of the constructed abyss, and it finally dawns on me.

Pater lied.

He never threw the boy down here, and I blindly followed my heart to save someone who wasn't even here to save.

CHAPTER EIGHTEEN

I don't know how long I've been down here. The sun has already set, which leads me to believe it's been a few hours, but I could be wrong. I don't know where Pater is either, and because I chose to defy him, I know he won't do a damn thing to help me if I can't reach the ladder.

I haven't tried yet. I'm too full of rage at myself for trying to be something I'm not and failing Vaughn yet again. Maybe he'll be better off if I just stay here. After all, the only thing I've managed to do is consistently fuck up every attempt I've made to help these boys, and because of it, one of them is already dead.

It would be so easy, almost too easy, for me to die right now. I could simply tie the end of the ladder around my neck and sit down, letting the weight of everything I've allowed to happen crush my neck.

I stand up and walk over, touching the tip of the ladder, and sigh. I deserve far worse than this, and that's the only thing that stops me.

That, and the hope that maybe Vaughn is alive out there somewhere. He's already deserted me by rebuking me as his mother, but I don't hate him for it. Had I been the one in his shoes being rejected at every turn, I would harbor the same feelings he does toward the "favorite."

I let go of the rope and sit back down on the cold, stone ground, wiping away bitter tears. There has to be some way to stop Pater; I just can't see it. I'm willfully blind to it because I need him as much as he needs me, even if it's not in the same way.

He wants to give me my own child, but then what? Will he do the same thing to me that he did to Mama if it's a girl? He said he'd never discard me, but what if that's the only way? To give him what he wants, pray for survival for the next fifteen years, and then allow him to finally end me when he takes the child as his new bride?

I've been in love with you since I first held you.

How is that possible? How can such a monster feel love for anything? And while I know I'm not better than Pater, I'm also not his equal. My love for the boys came from a need to protect them. The nights I've spent in Pater's bed, feeling his touch, were out of necessity, to keep them far from it.

I'm afraid part of my needing Pater is that I've learned to feel as much safety in his hands as I do down here in the darkness.

If there's an end to this, I can't see it; I don't *want* to see it. Maybe he'll be willing to come to some agreement of sorts, if what I have to offer is enough, but what can I give him that he hasn't already taken?

I rest my head back against the hard stone and almost laugh in relief. The answer is so clear to me, in a place where it's damn near impossible to see your own hand in front of your face. I *do* have something to offer Pater. Something he can't take unless I give it willingly, and it's the only way to get him to let his guard down.

With a renewed conviction, I get to my feet and wipe the dirt off on my legs before I reach up and begin to pull myself up the rope. I'm better at this than I should be. Even though I've spent countless nights out here alone, I've also had rare moments alone with Eloy and Vaughn when they've been able to sneak out unnoticed and throw the ladder down to me.

In a way, I feel like I'm clawing my way out of hell, and to be quite honest, maybe I am. The darkness no longer wants me because I'm no longer pure of heart. I have blood on my hands. Even though not spilled by my own hands, my misdeeds have caused the death of an innocent, and I'm being rejected by my safe place.

I understand it and I accept it.

I'll make my way back down here again once I've purged myself of that malady, and the only way to do it is to give myself completely and unconditionally to Pater.

I have to love him, *need* him, the way he loves me. It's the only way to earn his trust, and the simplest way to bring a tyrant to their knees. It's not an easy thing to topple an empire as an enemy, so I'll be his willing lover until the sun sets over the both of us for the last time.

CHAPTER NINETEEN

I decided to sleep in the clearing behind Pater's house. I don't want to give him the satisfaction of knowing where I am just yet, and I still have to convince myself that being his perfect little wife is worth the price I'll end up paying in the end.

I'm only awake now because the sun is breaking through the trees, and slivers of sunshine are hitting me in the face. I sit up with a sigh and look at the now empty stone chair. Eloy's mangled body is gone, and I'm sure Pater is the cause of it, but I can't worry about that now. He's not here to save anymore, and perhaps, in his brutal death, he's already received more salvation than I would have been able to provide for him anyway.

Today is the day I crawl out of my cocoon and become the delicate creature Pater has always longed for. The one he crushed when he decided Mama wasn't good enough for him anymore. The one he worked so vigilantly to destroy on the nights he needed to feel another's touch.

And I will become this. I've already decided it. The only thing I need to do now is stick to my plan and hope he doesn't see through me.

It shouldn't be too difficult, but I have to remember that I'm dealing with a master of deception, and he's more than likely already plucked the thoughts from my mind.

I lean down and scoop up one of the bloody stones, slip it into my shirt, and secure it safely so it has a place near my heart. It will serve as a reminder of why I will do these vile things I've committed myself to.

With the memory of Eloy tucked closely next to me, I make my way toward the back door of the house, and to my utter and complete fucking shock, feel like I've walked into an almost do over of a few days before.

There's a young woman and man I don't know standing on one side of the island in the kitchen. Pater is leaning against the counter, and Vaughn is sitting there quietly, speaking to her.

"There she is," he says with a warm smile, holding an arm out toward me. "This is my Jocelyn."

I walk dutifully over to him and let him wrap his arm around me, then turn and smile at the young couple who greet me with wide grins.

"Your dad was just telling us about you!" the young woman says brightly.

"My ... Dad?" I ask, stealing an

uncertain glance toward Pater. The stern look he returns to me tells me he's already rejected me. I've defied him one too many times, and when he's ready, I'll have to pay the price.

"From what he tells us, you seem like the perfect person we'd love to hire to babysit our son. Your brother said he's willing to help out too, if you need it," the young man explains, placing his palms on the island top with a smile.

"Oh. Yeah, I'd love to," I reply quietly.

"Joce will be an excellent babysitter. She helped raise her brother, and she hopes to be a mother herself one day, don't you baby girl?" he asks, giving me a gentle squeeze. Another stolen glance up into his eyes and I can see the soft yearning that was once going to play a part in my failed plan.

"I'd love to be a mom!" I gush happily. "How old is your son?"

"Seven," the young woman

replies with a smile. "He's our fur baby, but we still consider him our son, you know?"

"A dog?" I ask curiously.

They look at each other sheepishly and nod. A small smile curves my lips. I always wanted a pet, but Pater never allowed it for fear that the animal would attack him on the nights he attacked *me*.

"Can we bring him by tomorrow so you can meet him? He's really playful, so maybe a test run would be best before we commit," she says thoughtfully.

I turn and give Pater a hopeful glance, hoping it will soothe the anger I know he's feeling at the baby not being human, but he grunts and nods in agreement.

"Perfect! How does, say, seven o'clock sound?" the young man asks, glancing at Pater.

"That'll be just fine," he replies, in a bored tone.

With that, they shake hands with

Pater and wave at Vaughn and I as he shows them to the front door. I immediately go over to my brother and put a hand on his shoulder.

"I'm going to save you. I don't care if you hate me right now, but I need you to know that I'm going to do my best to fix this and that you'll go free," I whisper urgently.

Vaughn slowly turns his head toward me, his lower lip trembling, and bitter tears rolling down his face.

"Like you saved Eloy?" he seethes quietly.

I let out a sigh and do my best not to cry. If Pater finds us huddled in whispered conversation, he'll separate us again, and Heaven only knows if I'll see Vaughn ever again.

"Scheming against me?"

I jump and pull away from Vaughn, who turns his attention back to the void. There's nothing left in his eyes, like his brother's, but he still draws breath, and I will fucking defend it until I no longer can.

172

Pater is looking at us in amusement, arms over his chest, and his
grin sitting on his face. "I was
wondering when you were finally
going to crawl out of that fucking
hole."

"I'm sorry. I just needed some
time alone," I reply softly, clasping
my hands in front of myself.

Pater chuckles as he walks
toward us, stopping just short of
where I'm standing, and slides his
hand down my shirt. I try not to
cringe, but he knows that I'm holding
a piece of Eloy close to my heart and
he's more than likely not pleased
with the gesture.

"That doesn't belong there," he
says gently. "Hey. Kid. Get up. Go
back to where you were and stay
there until I come to get you."

Vaughn quickly scrapes his chair
back and leaves the room without so
much as a glance over his shoulder.
Pater lets out a sigh and rubs his forehead in irritation.

I watch his other hand as he absentmindedly rolls the stone around in his palm.

"You want this back?" he asks, following my gaze.

"Please."

"Tell you what," he says, as he begins to toss it from hand to hand. "I'll let you have it back if you do something for me."

I thought these fucking Tasks were over and done with.

"Anything," I say instead, remembering that I'm trying to become the obedient wife he wants me to be.

"Do a good job on your little interview tomorrow."

I raise an eyebrow at him. "That... That's it?"

"That's it," he replies with a nod.

"Okay," I say quietly, holding my hand out.

Pater balances the rock over my hand, but instead of dropping it where he promised, he closes his fist instead.

"I'm gonna hold on to this for a little while if you don't mind. I want to make sure you do a good job, if you catch my drift."

With that, he leans down and gently kisses me on the lips before he pulls back and grins again.

"Damn. Even after that stretch in the hole, your lips are still as soft as I remember."

Before I have a chance to plead for the rock, he leaves me in the kitchen, shaking his head and laughing on his way out.

CHAPTER TWENTY

I busy myself by tidying up the kitchen. I have a long day ahead of me, and once I'm done making this particular room spotless, I fully intend to go from room to room to locate Vaughn.

I take the dishtowel I've been using to wipe the island top with and toss it into the sink. I quickly turn the faucet on and off before I dry my hands on my legs and walk toward the living room. That's the direction Pater had gone, and I have to make sure I know where *he* is so that I have free reign of the house.

He's lying on the couch, the rock balanced on his stomach, and an arm bent behind his bed. The television is on, but it doesn't seem that he's paying it any mind.

"I was wondering when you were finally gonna join me," he says quietly. His eyes are trained on the screen, yet it's obvious he couldn't care less what's happening on the program he's watching.

"I'm sorry, Pater. I was just cleaning up."

"I know," he says kindly, closing his eyes. "Come sit with me, baby girl."

I swallow a sigh and obediently walk over so I can perch on the arm of the couch. Pater opens his eyes and turns them toward me, drops his legs, and motions with his chin for me to sit. As soon as I do, he props his legs across my lap and stares at me thoughtfully for a moment.

"Can I ask you something?"

It's a rhetorical question; he's the

only one that ever gets to ask questions or make statements without needing permission, but I nod anyway just to humor him.

"Alright. There's one thing that's irking the fuck out of me, and I'm hoping to get some clarity," he starts as he scratches his chin. "Do you love me because you want to, or because you feel you have to?"

I drape my hands over his legs and form my next words with deadly precision. "At first, I loved you because I felt I had to. If it weren't for you, I wouldn't be here." *Even if this is Hell, at least it's still something.* "But I think I'm learning to love you because it's what feels right."

Pater scoffs and shifts his legs on my lap. "Then why are you constantly plotting behind my back? At what point in this will you realize that I'll always know when you're trying to trick me, Jocelyn?"

I have to ask him. If I don't, it'll

drive me crazy for the little bit of life I know I have left.

"How is it you always know, Pater? I don't understand how it's possible to read the mind of another," I question, trying to keep the hysterics out of my tone. If he can hear the frantic need to know, he'll shut down and change the subject.

"How does a farmer always know their crops will spring from the ground? How does a gardener know that once a seed is planted, it'll eventually bloom? I *made* you, Jocelyn. You're a part of me, and I can feel you as deeply as you did with Eloy and Vaughn. It was never a trick, kiddo. Just an instinct, and you fucking fall for it every time," he explains with a smug smirk.

How could I have not guessed something so simple? It makes perfect sense.

I fold my arms and fall back against the couch, absolutely astounded at his revelation and the fact that I've been blind to it this entire time.

"Anything else you wanna know? Or is that enough for now?" he asks with a chuckle.

I turn my face away and sigh. The doorway stands empty, and I feel a heaviness in my heart. Usually, when I've been in this room with Pater, we were never alone. Eloy or Vaughn, or sometimes both, would be sitting by the door just to be close enough to me to feel some kind of comfort.

Pater swings his legs off the couch and sits up, moving until he's right next to me. He drapes an arm around my shoulders and sticks the rock with Eloy's blood on it into his pocket. I can feel his eyes on me, but I can't look at him yet. I feel the tears starting to build and I don't know if they're from anger at not seeing the boys where they should be, or because I was too fucking stupid not to have figured out his parlor trick sooner.

"Listen, I'm not going to make this harder than it has to be, and you really shouldn't either. I know this isn't the life you probably thought you would have, but honestly, Joce, would you have wanted to have it different in any way?" he asks, resting his free hand on my thigh. I look at his hand for a moment before I turn my eyes toward his.

"No," I reply quietly.

If it had been different, I never would have spent so many happy years with Eloy and Vaughn after Mama. I remember how often they would argue, and how much she would scream at him for loving someone that wasn't her. I just never knew it was *me* until the time came.

"Are you finally willing to work on this with me? We can be happy, you know. We'll even have a dog soon, and I know how much you've always wanted to have one of those," he says, giving me another gentle squeeze.

"Yes."

"Good girl," he says in relief, kissing my cheek. "Everything will work out, you'll see. For now, why don't you go get yourself cleaned up, and then I'll take you and your brother outside for a while, alright?"

"Okay. Thank you, Pater," I reply quietly as I shrink away from his arm and get to my feet.

"Hold on a second. How many times have I been inside you already? We're trying to start a family here, and 'Pater' won't do anymore. Not for you. Call me Luke," he offers, with a debonair smile.

Luke it is, I think with a sigh as I give him a small smile I return, before I walk away and leave him in his soon-to-be-short-lived moment of happiness.

CHAPTER TWENTY-ONE

I have a few more hours before the sun begins to set, yet I find myself standing in the doorway, wondering where Vaughn is tucked away. He's not in the darkness; I know this because Pater would never let him go outside alone. Any time the boys have been allowed a moment of fresh air, even with me being present, he would keep a watchful eye on us.

His footsteps have been moving about the house, hollowly echoing through the hallways, and for that reason alone, I know Vaughn is some-where inside with us.

I run a hand over my face and sigh irritably. This place is not exactly a palatial estate, so why I'm having such trouble figuring out where he is bothers me.

He's still alive. Half of my heart is still beating, and I know it's only because wherever he is, he hasn't been put to rest yet.

Don't think of things you can't control. That's one of Pater's rules; it's how he keeps his head above water, and those of us remaining under his thumb.

Leaning against the door frame, I watch the silent property. I don't know on which side of us the new couple lives, and to be honest, I didn't know it was possible for anyone to even be alive.

Besides Laura, we hadn't seen another person since we were kids, because Pater didn't want to take the chance we'd slip and tell stories of what we'd been subjected to under his roof.

I don't think I would ever tell anyone, even if do we make it out of here. I know nothing will come of it because the damage has already been done.

Stepping back inside, I close the door and sigh. Is it really damage, though? I can't say for sure, because there are nights when I've been in Pater's bed that his touch made all the difference in the world to me.

I'm as fucked up as he is; I can accept that now, but what I cannot accept is Vaughn being put through any more than he already has been. He's brutally murdered his own brother because I selfishly failed in my attempt to save him.

We all have blood on our hands now, and I can't help but wonder if that's what Pater had in mind all along. If we're all equally guilty, turning on him would essentially be turning on ourselves.

Monstrous acts beget monsters, and we'll both get what we deserve in the end, but not all of us. I won't allow it. Not while there's still hope for the boy to regain some sort of normalcy back into his life. He's only seventeen; he should be able to break away from all this madness if I can just help him escape.

Something tells me I don't have much time left to formulate a master plan, so I'll just have to improvise. The only chance I can actually see is when the couple returns with their dog. I'll have Pater sit with me while we have our interview. I'll play the part of the happy child, and I'll see to it that Vaughn can slip away unnoticed.

"Hey Joce?"

Pater's voice echoing throughout the house puts my plan to rest for the moment as I quickly turn and see that he's already heading toward me.

"What are you doing?" he asks with a curious smirk.

I shake my head and shrug. I

don't have an explanation he would appreciate, and since I know now that he can't really read my mind, I think my intentions are better left unsaid.

"Oh, I get it," he says kindly. "Alone time, right? I don't blame you. Even I need some of that every now and then. You hungry? I was thinking we could all sit down for dinner tonight. It's already going if you're interested."

"That would be nice," I reply softly.

"Good," he says with a warm smile. "Your brother is already in the dining room setting the table; why don't you go help him, and then you'll get to see what I whipped up."

Lowering my head, I start to walk past him, almost giddy with excitement. He's presenting me the chance I need to let Vaughn know that by this time tomorrow he could go free.

Pater slides an arm around my

waist as he pulls me sideways against him and rests his lips on the side of my head. He lingers there for a moment before he whispers a warning into my ear.

"Don't get any ideas. I'll find out."

He presses his lips gently against me in what I can only describe as a Judas kiss, because he betrayed me a long time ago when he stole my innocence. When he finally lets me go, I walk quickly toward the dining room. I need every second given to me to somehow get Vaughn to trust me.

As I walk into the room, I see that Vaughn is quietly setting Pater's plate at the head of the table. He glances up at me for a moment with his almost vacant eyes before he slowly walks to his seat and sits down.

"Listen to me, and don't interrupt until I'm done," I whisper as I take my place across from him. "I need you to trust me like you've never trusted me before. Tomorrow, you're leaving."

Vaughn raises his eyes from the plate he's been staring at, giving me an icy stare. "How is that, *Mom*?"

I try not to cringe. It's obvious he still hates me. I understand his feelings because I hate me too.

"When that couple comes back, I think we're going to do a working interview. Pater will be with me, I'll make sure of it. While I have them all distracted, I want you to walk out the front door and, no matter what happens, do *not* turn around, got it?" I ask him urgently.

Vaughn rolls his eyes, but he doesn't disagree with the plan. As long as Pater doesn't catch on to what's going to happen, he may actually do as he's being told.

"Doesn't this smell damn good?" Pater asks, suddenly walking into the room. He has a large serving plate piled with grilled chicken breasts that he sets down in the center of the table. My stomach growls loudly and I'm just now realizing how hungry I've been this entire time.

"It does," I reply, mustering the enthusiasm I know he's expecting.

Pater grins at me and turns his attention toward Vaughn, who's hungrily glancing at the plate. He quickly shoots Pater a glance and nods once in appreciation.

"But wait! There's more!" Pater says merrily as he leaves the room again.

It's another form of discipline, sitting in front of the food, raven-ously hungry, and not being allowed to indulge until Pater says so. Of course, it's also very far and few in between that he allows us to share in his food that, when presented with the challenge, we've always held strong.

He returns a few moments later

with a bowl heaped with mashed potatoes, balancing a bottle of wine under his arm, and still grinning. He's proud of himself for actually giving a fuck about us for once.

"Want some?" he asks, as he pulls the cork out of the wine bottle. I glance at him to see who he's asking, and am actually surprised to find it's me, since I've never tasted wine before.

He fills his glass, then moves the bottle toward mine, hovering, waiting for my response. Will it dull my senses? Will I divulge my plan if I imbibe? I don't know, and I can't take that chance.

"No thank you, Pater," I reply softly.

"Luke," he corrects, the grin on his face faltering. He turns his gaze toward Vaughn. "What about you, kid?"

"No thank you, sir," he says quietly.

Pater shrugs and sets the bottle down by his glass and rolls his sleeves up to his elbows. "Well, more for me then. Jocelyn, can you pass the chicken please?"

I immediately pick up the plate and hold it out toward him. His grin is fully plastered on his face again as he uses a fork to take the biggest piece, then winks at me when he's done. I hold it out toward Vaughn, who quickly stabs whatever piece he can get, then nods in thanks.

Pater reaches past me and grabs the bowl of mashed potatoes, purposely rubbing his bare forearm against mine. I don't react because I'm not sure what reaction he's looking for.

"Eat up kids, tomorrow's a big day. We're getting a dog," he says with a laugh.

I raise my eyes toward Vaughn, but he's too busy shoving forkfuls of food into his face to care or notice.

"Oh, I almost forgot," Pater says conversationally. "I never did get a chance to thank you for taking care of that little problem your brother left behind, Vaughn."

Vaughn's mouth is open, and his fork is hovering just in front of him. He glances at Pater, then cuts his eyes toward me frantically. They're hiding something from me, and Pater doesn't like it when we keep secrets from each other.

"Didn't he tell you?" he asks in mock surprise as he cuts a piece of chicken with his fork.

I feel sick. Without even knowing what he's about to reveal to me, I've lost my fucking appetite and my body begins to tremble slightly.

"Tell me what?" I croak uncertainly.

He lets his fork clatter loudly onto his plate as he sits back and takes a sip of his wine. "Well? Are you going to tell her, or am I?"

Vaughn turns his face away from me and Pater chuckles. "I swear, I don't know how the hell you ended up being my kid with no balls."

"Tell me *what?*" I ask again.

"Alright," Pater says, placing an arm on the table and looking at me. He stops for a moment to take another sip of wine before he makes his revelation. "Remember how I said your mother went out of this world the same way she came in?"

"Yes?"

The world is starting to spin around me. I'm dangerously close to passing out, but it's the anticipation of what I think he might say that's making me react so violently.

"Well, your precious Mama? Her name was Laura. You got to meet her. And the blood she went out in? That was Eloy's; sloppy as fuck, cut himself a couple times doing the deed. But don't feel bad, you didn't really miss anything spectacular. The bitch didn't even put up a fight."

Clearing his throat, he takes another sip of wine and then continues with his meal. My mother was here, in this very house, not a few days before; she did nothing to save us.

CHAPTER TWENTY-TWO

Dinner has officially been over for half an hour, but Pater has insisted on dessert. For himself, not us; we haven't earned dessert yet, according to him.

"But you will," he promised us with his sideways grin sitting deviously on his handsome face.

It's been silent for at least ten minutes while Pater eats his pie, but I'm so numb at the revelation he made to me less than an hour ago that I'll probably end up staying awake all night anyway.

"Listen, I know you're all

confused and probably pissed off right now," he finally says, glancing at me. "But Vaughn didn't really know until he had to go clean up Eloy's mess. And to be honest Joce, you can't be angry at me. That waste of a pussy has lived in this neighborhood ever since I kicked her out. She could've come over any time she wanted. Well, that's not entirely true, but if she was as concerned as she fucking acted, then she *would* have."

Pater's words mean nothing to me. I'm too busy glancing at the knife sitting between us. All it would take is a series of quick motions to leave him choking in his own blood. I could slit his throat before he would even have the chance to realize what had happened.

But what if I failed? What if he managed to stop me as soon as I grabbed the knife? Then what? Vaughn would surely pay for another act of failed bravery. And then it would just be Pater and me.

Unless...

"You know Joce, I admire you," Pater says suddenly. "You've got more balls than either of your brothers, always looking for a way to kill me and whatnot, but I thought we agreed we were done with that game?"

My eyes slowly move from the gleaming blade to the hilt, and then up to Pater. Out of the corner of my eye, I can see Vaughn slowly moving for the knife placed between him and Pater, and in that moment, I know it's a trick.

"Don't," I say to him softly.

Pater raises his eyebrows curiously as he turns his attention toward Vaughn, who's letting go of the knife.

"You kids really like to test my patience, don't you?" Pater asks with a sigh. "It's okay. If it were me, I'd try the same thing, but remember something. Without me, you're both nothing. You'll be forced out into a world you don't understand; a world that will reject you before you can even set a foot firmly into it. I'm not the bad guy here. I'm not the one who threw you kids away; I'm the one who's loved you and cared for you your entire lives. You want someone to hate? Hate your incubator. She gave all three of you up without a fight."

Vaughn puts his face in his hands and begins to gently cry. He believes Pater, and it's breaking his heart. He believes there's nothing better than this life for the both of us, and he can't accept it like I've been trying to.

Pater rolls his eyes at Vaughn before turning his attention back to me. "Tell you what; to prove I'm not such a bad guy, I'll do something for the both of you. Tonight, I'm going to let you sleep with your brother."

My stomach turns, because with Pater, the way he says things are rarely as they're presented. He looks very proud because of his generosity, but I won't thank him just yet. Not until I fully understand his offer.

"Calm down, will you?" he says with a chuckle, reaching across the table and resting a hand on mine. "I meant actually let you sleep in the same bed, not fuck each other. That would just complicate things. Besides, that's not how this works. Your pussy belongs to me and no one else, so don't worry about it."

Somehow, that doesn't make me feel any better. If he's allowing this, it means the worst is yet to come, and he's giving us a peaceful moment before the end.

"Thank you, Pater," I finally say softly.

"Luke," he corrects evenly.

"Thank you, Luke," I correct with a sigh. "Where would you like us to sleep tonight?"

"Anywhere you want," he says, his grin returning as he pushes his chair back and stands up. "But remember; no funny business. That would be wrong."

With a wink, he grabs his plate and leaves us in the dining room. My eyes move toward the clock on the wall, and I'm amazed at how much time has actually passed since we've sat down. It's eight o'clock at night, maybe a little after, and as I look across the table at my brother, I can't help but feel like this is the last time I'll ever see him again.

"Come on," I say quietly, getting up from the table and holding a hand out toward him. "Let's get some sleep. Tomorrow, you're getting out of here."

CHAPTER TWENTY-THREE

When I wake up the next morning, I'm relieved to realize I didn't dream. It's not uncommon for me to have sleepless dreams, but when I do, they terrorize me. They're almost always dreams of life outside these walls. A life without Pater; one where Eloy is still alive, and he and Vaughn are happy and thriving.

Since Pater had given me the choice of rooms, I chose the one I slept in as a little girl, yet untouched and undefiled because it still held some meaning to me. It was a place where I could go and be innocent again; a place where Pater didn't exist, and nothing bad could happen to me.

I blink my eyes a few times to remove whatever sleep is still lingering and smile sadly when I feel his frail body so close to mine. When we went to bed, I held him while he cried, until he was so exhausted he finally drifted off. I've woken up with his head under my chin and his arms still wrapped firmly around me.

He's stirring slightly since I've shifted in bed, and I kiss the top of his head. I don't want him to wake up just yet. I want to remember him like this before he leaves me. Asleep, innocent of the horrors he's lived through, and finding it in himself to forgive me, even if he doesn't mean it.

I run my hand gently over his hair as he stirs again gently before he finally opens his eyes and pulls away from me.

"What time is it?" he asks groggily, using the back of his hand to rub

his eyes. Before I have a chance to
answer him, the door swings open,
and Pater walks through.

"Get up and get dressed; they're
here."

"Now?" I ask, sitting up, now
wide awake.

"Yeah," he replies with a grim
nod. "Hurry up."

"Fuck," I mutter pushing myself
off the bed. "Okay, listen, go throw
some water on your face and get as
alert as you can."

I walk quickly toward my closet
and pull out a dress, changing
quickly behind the door so Vaughn
doesn't have to be subjected to any
more than he already has been.
When I'm done, I get up onto my
tiptoes and run my hand along the
top shelf.

"Here, take this," I say, walking
back toward him and shoving all the
money I managed to save as a child
into his hand. "It's not much, but it
should get you far enough away from

here that you won't ever have to worry about this place again. I love you, okay? Don't ever forget that. I love you."

I give him a quick, tight hug, and walk out of the room before he can say anything. If I hear anything come from his lips, I'll burst into tears and fail the interview, and he won't have his chance.

He'll take it.

He has to, because he knows that life *is* better on the outside, no matter what Pater tried to tell us last night. Maybe one day I'll see him in the world; maybe I won't ever leave these walls. The latter doesn't matter to me because I know I deserve this, but goddamn it, he doesn't.

"There she is," Pater says with a huge, fake smile when I walk into the living room. "Crystal and Aaron were just asking about you."

"Sorry!" I reply as brightly as I can. "I guess I overslept. I honestly thought you guys meant seven o'clock at *night*."

"Oh, he's an early riser," Aaron says, nodding down at his dog. It's got beautiful brown fur that shines majestically as it sits there looking up at me curiously. I don't know what kind of dog it is, but it's definitely friendly. As I approach it and crouch down to pet its head, I can see the tail begin to wag furiously.

"What's your name?" I ask him, scratching behind his ear.

"Tiberius," Crystal replies with a warm smile.

I raise an eyebrow curiously at her as Tiberius licks the side of my face.

"I know; what kind of name is that for a dog, right? We're really big into ancient history," she explains with a laugh.

I smile at her and turn my attention back to the dog, taking its face into my hands and giving it a gentle kiss on the nose.

"He definitely seems to like you," Aaron says happily. "Wanna sit down and we'll talk about compensation?"

I have no idea what that means, but I pet Tiberius one more time, before I get up and go sit next to Pater on the couch.

"We're going to be gone for a couple of weeks, which I guess we should have told you ahead of time," Crystal begins sheepishly. "If it's still okay with your dad, we'd love to have you take care of him for us while we're gone."

As I'm turning my eyes toward Pater, I can see Vaughn quietly walking past the living room door. He's doing it; he's leaving, and he's going to have a happy life.

"Daddy?" I ask, glancing at Pater. I want to keep his attention. I want him to focus on me because as long as he's distracted by my hand on his leg and the sound of my voice, everything will work out as I hoped it would.

"I don't know," he finally says, shaking his head slowly. "Two weeks is a long time to take care of a dog for someone that's never had one. Are you sure you're up for that kind of responsibility?"

"I've done a good job so far, haven't I?" I ask him through gritted teeth and a forced smile.

He returns my fake smile, but I can see the stern warning plainly in his eyes. "Yes, you have."

"Well, if you're still willing to accept the job, we'll pay you two hundred dollars. One hundred now, and one hundred when we get back. Does that sound fair?" Aaron asks, putting an arm around Crystal.

"We have all his stuff outside in the car too, so you won't have to use any of your money to buy him food or toys," Crystal adds hopefully.

"Sweetheart?" Pater asks, putting

his arm around my shoulders and giving me a squeeze.

"I would love to!"

They both smile in relief and get to their feet. "We'll just go outside and get his belongings then!"

"Wait!" I say quickly. What if they go outside and Vaughn is still within the line of vision? "Um. Maybe you'd like to see where he's going to sleep first?"

"Oh, I'm sure he'll sleep fine wherever you decide to put him," Aaron says cheerfully as he walks out of the living room with Crystal following behind him. He still has Tiberius' leash firmly wrapped in his fist, and I'm afraid I'm going to piss myself because of how scared I am right now.

But as I begin to follow them out, Pater firmly holding my hand in his, I see something that causes me to almost pass out. I fall against Pater, who tries to steady me, and I swear to

God, the world is starting to go black around me.

"Hey. I thought you guys might need some help."

Vaughn is standing dutifully next to their car, waiting for someone, anyone to come outside, so he can do what he always has tried to do best.

Protect us from Pater. And since he bears the guilt of not being able to save his brother, he's going to try to save me.

CHAPTER TWENTY-FOUR

"What are you doing out here?" Pater asks him with a menacing smile now sitting on his face.

Vaughn shrugs as he meets my eyes, "I wanted to see the dog. I didn't know it was already inside."

I blink my eyes rapidly as I do my damnedest not to cry. The plan would have worked so perfectly if he would have just kept walking. He could have left this all behind, but because he still holds some kind of love in his heart for me, he won't leave me behind.

"Go on inside, son. We'll have a

little talk later," Pater says, squeezing my shoulders tightly enough to cause me to flinch. He knows I had a hand in this, but he can't act on his rage until our company is gone.

Vaughn nods and pets Tiberius' head as he walks by him, stealing a glance in my direction. I look at him with more heartbreak than I ever thought I could feel in my life, and he responds with a sad smile before disappearing into the house.

Aaron quickly unloads the dog's belongings and carries them into the living room, before pulling out his wallet and handing me a crisp one hundred dollar bill. He and Crystal say their goodbyes to the dog, shake Pater's hand, and wave at me as they get back into their car and begin to pull down the driveway.

"Joce?" Pater asks thoughtfully.

I glance up at him, trying to shrug out of the grip he has on me. Tiberius is inside playing with Vaughn; I know it because I can hear him happily barking and Vaughn returning it with laughter. For the first time in years, Vaughn is genuinely laughing again, and the purity of it slightly swells my deflated heart.

"What your brother just did. Was that his idea or yours?"

"Mine. It was completely, unequivocally my idea. Please don't punish him for it. Please? I'll go back into the oubliette. I'll rot down there happily, but please. He didn't want to go; I forced him outside."

I'm damn near hysterical as I pull away from the grip he has on my shoulders. I turn to face him and ball his shirt into my fists, looking up at him with pleading eyes, but he's more focused on the car.

Waiting for it to disappear from sight.

Waiting for the moment he can strike us down for what we attempted to do.

Waiting for things he'll never say.

Pater won't waste words when actions can be taken instead, and I'm afraid. Not for myself, but for Vaughn.

Why didn't he leave?!

I fall against Pater's chest and begin sobbing. He won't care; my tears never meant much to him before, and they aren't even for him. They're not for myself either; they're for the innocent inside who will suffer because I tried to help him.

"Let's go inside," he says quietly, putting his arm around me and leading me back in. He hasn't agreed not to hurt the boy, but I hope that somewhere deep down in the void where his soul *should* be, he'll take some pity on him and allow me to take the punishment in his place.

Once inside, he firmly closes the door and turns both the locks deliberately. He turns the doorknob to make sure it's locked, before leading me into the living room where Tiberius and Vaughn are still playing.

"Go sit on the floor with your brother," Pater says, damn near shoving me down next to Vaughn. Tiberius, blissfully unaware of what he might see, comes over and licks my face.

Not now, I think, giving him a gentle shove. He looks at me curiously, before he trots out of the room to explore the rest of the house.

Pater sits down on his couch and puts his face in his hands for a moment, trying to collect his thoughts before he speaks. If a verbal lashing is the worst of what he has to offer, I'll gladly accept it.

"I know you both hate me, but you also know that I don't care. I have rules for a reason, and that's to protect you both. Your brother couldn't follow the fucking rules, and do you see where that got him? Dead at thirteen years old, when he could have still been here with us. You have had it way too easy, and that's gonna fucking change, starting now," he says, dropping his hands and glaring at us.

Easy? This is easy? Being forced to play the dutiful wife to your father; being forced to protect your brothers, and failing where it counts the most?

I don't dare speak those sentiments out loud. No matter how much I want to stand up and scream my questions at him, I stay seated and move closer to Vaughn. I can feel him trembling when he puts a protective arm around my shoulders, but his attempt to reassure me is such an act of bravery in the face of this evil that I can't help but feel proud.

I may not have made many good decisions in my life, and I may have gotten a lot of shit wrong, but I know that at the very least, I raised him right.

Pater leans back against the couch and stares at us with his mouth open. He's just warned us of what's to come, and yet here we sit in solidarity against a tyrant.

He chuckles as he looks away for a moment. I can see the wheels spinning in his head and I'm ready for whatever it is he decides to put us through next, because I'll have Vaughn by my side. With as much as I wanted him to gain his freedom, being in his presence makes me feel stronger.

"If only you cared this much about Eloy. Maybe then he'd still be alive, too," Pater says to me with a smirk. He's trying to hurt me, devastate me with his words, and if I still didn't have one son to care for, I would have felt the blow much harder, just as he intended.

"She did, and that's why she couldn't kill him," Vaughn retorts bravely.

I put a hand on his leg to keep him from talking back to Pater, but he must be working on pure adrenaline because he hops to his feet and balls his fists at his side.

"You're not as great as you think

you are. You can beat us, throw us into the ground, abuse Jocelyn as much as you want; but you'll never be more than a monster. If you were as great as you act like you are, you wouldn't do this to us," he shouts at him.

"Wow. Look at you go!" Pater says in appreciation. "I see your balls finally dropped. Congratulations, kid!"

I don't know where my sudden bravery comes from. Maybe it's seeing my younger brother stand up and not give a shit about the conse-quences of speaking back to Pater, but I get up, stand next to him, and place a hand gently on his shoulder.

"You can leave now. Walk out the front door like I told you to, and don't look back. He can't hurt you anymore, Vaughn. You just took control of your life again. It's okay. I'll be okay," I say to him softly.

"I'm not leaving you here with *him*," he replies, his eyes still on

Pater, who's watching us with sheer amusement on his face.

"Please let him leave," I beg, giving Pater my full attention. "I'll stay for as long as you want me to, and die when you deem it necessary, but he's been through enough. If you love me as much as you say you do, you'll let him go."

Pater smiles and rubs his chin. He gets up and faces us but doesn't make any steps to come closer. I can tell he's mulling my request over by the way he's looking me up and down. He's trying to decide whether I'll be enough to keep him satisfied, and if he gives me the chance, I'll do every last thing he asks of me.

"Tell you what," he begins as he rubs his hands together. The look in his eyes is sickening, but no matter what he says, I will fucking oblige to keep Vaughn free from whatever torment he decides to inflict.

"I'll make sure that Vaughn goes free, but you *both* have to do something for me first," he says, grinning widely.

I shake my head vehemently.

"Hear me out before you say no, otherwise you both go back into the ground until you die of starvation."

"It's okay," Vaughn says, taking my hand in his. I look at him and he gives me a small but firm smile. "What do you want?"

Pater smiles at him as he claps his hands together. "Go get the dog and bring it back in here. One little thing I want you kids to do, and then I'll let you go."

Vaughn nods in agreement as he lets go of my hand and leaves me alone in the room with Pater, whose grin is making me feel violently ill.

One more fucking game and Vaughn will be able to leave.

CHAPTER TWENTY-FIVE

Pater's whistling while we wait for Vaughn to return with Tiberius, and I'm still firmly standing my ground. I can't even begin to imagine what he has in store for us; nor do I want to, but I won't resist whatever it is with the price being Vaughn's chance at a normal life.

"Where do you think he would have gone to?" Pater asks me, a curious smile replacing his wicked grin.

"I don't know."

"Where did you tell him to go?" he asks, rocking back on his heels.

"I didn't. I only told him to run as far away as he could and to not look back," I reply truthfully.

"Hm," he says with a nod. "I don't know if he would have gotten very far, but you did one hell of a job distracting me. That 'Daddy' thing got me hard for a minute there."

I sigh and clasp my hands firmly in front of me. The kind of fucked up thoughts that run through his head were absolutely beyond me, but I can honestly say that I no longer care.

"There they are," he says, turning his attention toward the door. "I got a question for you before we start," he says to Vaughn. "Where exactly where you planning on going?"

Vaughn drops down to one knee and proceeds to unclip the leash from Tiberius' collar, giving Pater a shrug in return.

"Away."

"'Away'. Okay, well I'll make sure you make your way there after we're done. But first, you gotta do something for me, remember?"

Vaughn glares up at him from his place next to Tiberius and begins to get to his feet when Pater walks over and shoves him back down. "You're not gonna need to stand for this."

My heart begins to race. The first time Pater ever said that to me, what followed next was the metaphorical wildfire that destroyed my garden.

"Wait--"

"Ah, ah, ah!" Pater says holding up a finger. "You promised."

I stand frozen in horror as he pulls his shirt off, revealing his body underneath. Pater may be much older than us, but he takes good care of himself. He's not by any means chiseled out of stone, but what he has to offer would be appreciated by someone else in the right situation.

"Sit down, baby girl. Take your clothes off and spread your legs. Let me see that sweet little pussy."

My lower lip begins to tremble

violently as I remove my pants and panties and sit on the floor. Closing my eyes for a moment, I turn my face away as I slowly spread my legs open, praying that Vaughn is looking away.

"God, I can smell you from here," he remarks, inhaling deeply. My eyes fly open when I hear him begin to unzip his jeans, and I can feel myself dangerously close to vomiting. He's going to fuck me and make Vaughn watch, and he'll have this burned in his memory forever, losing his chance at a normal life.

"Nobody move. I just got an idea," he says with a smirk, as he walks out of the room. Moments later, he returns with the largest kitchen knife he has, and walks back over toward Vaughn.

Instinct tells me to get up and try to wrestle the knife away from him, but the very second he sees the fight in my eyes, he grabs a fistful of the boy's hair and pulls his head back, placing the blade against it.

"Do you really want to do that? Now? Before we've had fun?" he asks with a slight bounce in his stance and that fucking grin on his face. I sit back down on my bare ass and watch the blade carefully. Not only is it the largest, it's also the sharpest, and even the slightest pressure will draw blood.

"Now let's play, shall we?" he says, violently shoving Vaughn back to his knees. "I know you'll like this because of how badly you wanted to take care of that fucking thing. So spread your legs again for me."

I'm crying at this point. There's no more reason to be brave when I'm so sure I know what he's going to do to me.

"Feel that?" he asks Vaughn, rubbing himself against the side of the boy's face. "That's what happens when your balls drop. Ever happen to you before?"

Vaughn tries to move away from

Pater, who promptly reaches down and grabs a fistful of his hair again.

"I guess not. It's okay, you're not gonna need a hard dick for what I want you to do," he says with a chuckle. "Now, let's start, and if you bite me, I'll fucking gut your sister. Got it?"

Oh my God.

"Pater, no!"

"Call me Pater one more fucking time and I'll cut your precious brother's head off his fucking neck," he shouts at me. "Get busy with that fucking dog and let me enjoy myself here."

Vaughn and I exchange a wide-eyed, horrified glance. We understand now, and what he wants is far worse than anything he's ever put me through. But it doesn't stop him; nothing stops Pater when he really wants something.

Balancing the knife in the same hand he's still using to hold Vaughn by his hair, he pulls out his hard dick and shoves it into the boy's mouth, moving back and forth violently, gagging him with a grin on his face.

"Come on. Find your own pace and it won't be so bad," he says to him in a thick voice.

Tiberius is sitting next to me, watching the entire scene unfold curiously, his head tilted to the side, and I don't know what to do at this point. I don't know exactly what it is that Pater expects from me, and I'm so horrified by what he's forcing Vaughn to do that I throw up all over the carpet.

"Hm, that's good," he says, leaning his head back and closing his eyes. "It's not so bad now, is it?"

I have to improvise. I have to do something, *anything*, that will bring this to the fastest end possible. I quickly grab Tiberius by the collar and shove his snout between my legs, rubbing my pussy against his nose until he begins to lick curiously. His tongue is wide, flat, coarse, and I hate every fucking minute of it, but I have to give Pater something so that Vaughn can be free of what he's being subjected to.

"How's that feel, baby girl?" he asks, opening his eyes and looking down at me. "Is he better than me?"

My jaw is clenched so tightly together that I swear my goddamn teeth are going to start chipping soon, but when the dog attempts to pull back, I move forward and shove myself back into his face.

Tiberius finally begins to growl, and I know it's time to stop. I don't want this poor animal to be treated like we are; I want it to feel loved and cared for, not abused, and broken, so I let it go and walk quickly over to Pater and Vaughn. I put my hands on my brother's shoulders and attempt to pull him out of Pater's grip, but Pater only laughs and shoves me away.

"You didn't finish. I guess it didn't know what it was doing, cause you *always* finish with me, don't you?" he asks, pulling me as close as he can and looking down into my eyes.

"Yes," I reply frantically, darting my eyes back down toward Vaughn, who's gasping for air in between tears.

"Is that all you got? The both of you? That's a damn shame," Pater says, finally pushing Vaughn off his dick. "I did promise you that I would let Vaughn go though, didn't I? And Daddy always keeps his promises to his sweet girl," he says, reaching down and grabbing my ass tightly. "Step back. I don't want you to get hurt."

I take three shaky steps back and wait. Any moment now, Vaughn will be allowed to get to his feet and walk out the front door, just like it was agreed upon.

"Come here, kid," he says to Vaughn as he puts his dick back into his pants, careful not to nick himself with the knife. "You about ready to go?"

Vaughn is sobbing so violently at this point that he can't form a cohesive sentence. Pater rolls his eyes and reaches for him again.

"You sure you wanna leave?" he asks him. He doesn't wait for a response though. Instead, he shoots me a quick smile, before he turns his attention back to the boy. "Alright, go on, you get to go now. Tell your brother we said hey," he says, as he pulls Vaughn's head back, cleanly and deeply cutting his neck wide open.

All I can do is scream and watch as his hands fly up toward his neck, the warm blood rushing over his fingers before he finally pitches forward and bleeds out on the living room carpet.

He's finally free.

CHAPTER TWENTY-SIX

"Damn. I really wanted you to do that, but I'm pretty sure you weren't up for it, were you?" Pater asks as he tilts his head and glances down at Vaughn. The boy isn't dead yet; I can hear him still gasping for breath and I can see his back moving raggedly up and down. "Wanna finish him off? Put him out of his misery?"

Pater turns the knife around so that he's gripping the blade in his hand and presenting the hilt to me. It's another test, and it's one I cannot afford to fail. Being forced to do something so terrible in a moment where my heart can't take any more, I turn my face away from Pater and reject his request.

"Don't have it in you, huh? It's okay, let him suffer for a little bit. It'll teach him a lesson before he chokes to death on his own blood," he says as he crosses his arms and shakes his head.

He uses his foot to nudge Vaughn's shoulder, which causes him to sputter, and I hate myself for not having it in me to kill him. But it's what Pater wants, and I can't give in, not when I've already given him so fucking much already.

"Hey, where did that mutt run off to?" he asks, suddenly glancing around the room.

"No more," I whisper tiredly. "I can't do this anymore. Please just end it."

"Nah, I'm having too much fun, and you're not pregnant with my child yet," he replies with smirk. "We've got things to do first, baby girl. Then if you want to leave, we'll talk about it, but as it currently stands, I have no plan of letting you go. Besides, do you have any idea how cute you're gonna look with a belly? I'll bet it's gonna be adorable! Can I tell you a secret, though?"

I don't move my hands away from my face. I won't give him the satisfaction of seeing more tears, when I didn't even know I was capable of giving any more than I've already shed.

"I'm trying to share something with you. Please give me a little common courtesy," he says quietly as he walks over and pulls my hands away. Pater tries to catch my eyes, but I still refuse, causing him to sigh impatiently.

"Jocelyn. Stop acting like a spoiled brat and look at me when I'm speaking to you, please."

I turn my eyes ever so slightly to let him know he has my attention as much as he has my defiance, but he seems to be okay with it.

"I'm a little scared. To start over, I mean. Fifty three years on this fucking earth and having to raise another kid from scratch is gonna be a little hard, so I'm counting on you to help me with that. Although to be honest, I bet changing a diaper is a lot like getting back on a bike; you never really forget. I remember the first time I changed yours; the way you looked up at me with those curious brown eyes..." his voice trails off and he pulls me close to him protectively, resting his chin on the top of my head.

If I didn't know any better, I would say he's almost trying to remember how to be a father in this moment, but I know it won't last long. It never fucking does, and I'll be back to being his wife in no time while our 'son' continues to bleed out on the floor next to us.

"It won't be anything like it was

with your mom, so don't worry about that, okay? I took you kids away from her the moment you were born, because I could see in her eyes how much she resented you. I didn't appreciate the way she would look at you, especially. Which is probably why you kids didn't remember her when you saw her; you were never around her long enough to form that bond, because I refused to give her that right to *my* children," he takes a deep breath to steady himself. I can feel the rage in his words, but he's trying to make this as meaningful as he can for me. "Listen, I fully intend to raise our kids together instead of apart. I've seen how hard you tried with Eloy and Vaughn, and it would break my heart to take you away from any child I put inside of you. You're a damn good mother, Jocelyn, of that I have no doubt," he says, as he kisses the top of my head and lets me go. "But for now, we gotta find that fucking dog."

He walks out of the room, whistling loudly in an attempt to get Tiberius to show himself, but if he can hear him he's not falling for it.

Good dog. Stay as far away as you fucking can.

"Luke?" I call out timidly. I have another plan, one that won't fail if I can stand my ground. One that will, at the very least, save the life of the animal if I can keep his attention on me long enough.

"Not now, baby girl. I need to get rid of this damn dog," he calls back before he continues whistling. "There you are! Come here, boy! That's right, I've got something for you."

I run from the living room, down the hallway, and into the kitchen. Pater has the dog by his collar, and he's crouched down in front of him, letting Tiberius happily lick his face.

"Well, look at that. I can almost taste your pussy when he does that," he remarks as he glances back at me with a laugh. Tiberius continues to lick Pater's face until he pulls away from him. "Alright, that's about enough of that. Now, you really didn't think I was going to let you violate my wife and not punish you, did you?"

"What? Luke, he doesn't know any better. I forced myself on him, he didn't do anything to me. I swear! Please, I'll open the door and he can run away, and I'll tell Aaron and Crystal that it was my fault he's gone. I'll give them their money back and maybe they'll forgive me. Okay? You don't have to punish him; punish me, okay?" I plead, ringing my hands nervously.

"Hm. It's a tempting offer, but if I can't resist putting my face in between your thighs, what's to say he won't try it again?" he asks, turning his attention back to Tiberius. "I think he'll be okay after this."

Pater pushes the dog down firmly. I move forward to try and stop him, but it's too late. Tiberius lets out a loud yelping noise as Pater drives the blade under his chin, up through the top of his head.

"I always did like animals," he says, more to himself than me, as he turns the blade viciously so that the dog doesn't suffer any more than it needs to. "Just not this one."

CHAPTER TWENTY-SEVEN

Numb doesn't begin to describe how I feel anymore. I'm hollow, empty, void of life, and yet here I stand watching Pater as he turns the dog onto its back and splits it open. He's talking to me, telling me how he'll skin the dog and make a blanket for our newborn child when we have one, but his voice is so distorted that I'm sure I've lost most of his words in translation. Or maybe this is all just a bad dream, and I'll wake up in a world where it all starts at the beginning and never makes it this far.

I turn away from what he's doing

and wrap my arms around myself as I walk back into the living room. Vaughn is dead at this point; his back is no longer moving up and down, and as I walk over and place a hand gently on his back, I can feel him starting to become cold to the touch. The sweet peach colored skin that once shown so warmly on him before our lives became this Hell, is slowly turning a soft shade of pale. I know that when it's over, he'll be bitter blue and no amount of trying to keep his body warm will make him the beautiful boy he used to be again.

"I'm sorry, my sweet boy," I whisper, leaning down and kissing the top of his head. I pull my shirt off over my head and lay it across his stiffening body. It's not much, but it's the only comfort I can offer to him now.

I think I can hear Pater calling out my name, but I continue my pilgrimage slowly toward the front door, walking out and around the house.

While it would have been much easier to walk out the back door, I would have had to walk past Pater to get there, and I can't stand the sight of him anymore. His bitter tongue has told enough lies that I would prefer to leave this fucking world without hearing any more false promises of how good a life is yet to come.

I push my way through the brushes, the low hanging branches, acquiring more scrapes than I ever have in the oubliette, but I don't care. Eloy is out here somewhere, and I have to say goodbye to him.

When I make it into the clearing, I can see that his body is even more mangled than before, and he's toppled off the throne. I assume wild animals have gotten to him, though it won't deter me from giving my youngest the same gentle kiss I gave to his brother. I loved them both equally, and I still do; even if they went to their deaths believing otherwise, I hope they knew in their hearts that my love for them never faltered.

I pull his body toward the center of the clearing and turn him onto his back. Brushing his hair off his face, I lean down and kiss his forehead. Had I been strong enough to end him when commanded, his death would have been so much easier than it became.

I'll always owe Eloy a debt I cannot repay, but I'll find a way to make it right in the next life. Maybe he'll smile at me when he sees me; maybe it'll be his turn to throw stones. Either way, I just hope to God he doesn't hate me for all that's happened to him.

I wish I knew where Laura was. Pater hid her body so well that I'll never be able to say goodbye to her. I can't hate her for what's happened to us; as much as I want to, I understand now. She didn't have a choice in what happened, and she probably didn't realize how evil Pater was until it was too late.

Getting back to my feet, I look up through the trees and sigh.

"I'm sorry, Mom. I know you tried," I whisper into the oblivion. "It ends with me; I promise."

I can hear Pater again. He's outside. His footsteps are fast approaching because he knows I'd come out here. I don't answer him, instead taking in the last few peaceful moments I can with the one I've wronged the most.

Lowering myself to the ground, I turn my body toward Eloy and wrap an arm around him, as I close my eyes and wait for a well-deserved death to be bestowed upon me.

PATER

"What have I told you about going near the well?"

I walk over and pick up my daughter, laughing as her light brown pigtails brush against my face. The sound of her laughter is what keeps me going; that and knowing that she loves me as unconditionally as I love her. She doesn't see a monster, she sees a father, and that's how it should be.

"You're too curious for your own good," I chide her kindly, giving her a kiss on the cheek. She smiles widely in return, and I can't help but laugh, because I know that smile all too fucking well.

Laughing, she pushes my face away. It's the stubble against their smooth skin that always gets them. For the most part, anyway, because I have no intention of making this one my wife. I want to play the part of the dutiful father for a while. I want to make sure that she has a good upbringing, and that she never hears about her good-for-nothing brothers and grandmother.

Nah, I'll tell her all about what a good life those three had if she ever asks about them, which I don't know why she would. I never had any pictures of any of them, so it would only be word of mouth, and there's no one around to fill her head with lies against me.

She would never believe it. She only knows me as a good daddy because that's what I am. I'm the best fucking father she'll ever have, and I was to my other kids, too; they just chose to always see the bad side of shit.

"Why do you keep coming out here, huh?" I ask her with a smile.

I don't want to think about the past anymore. It's not gonna do anything but put me in a shitty mood, and she deserves better from me.

"Wanna take a better look? Come on, hold on tightly to Daddy, and I'll show you what's down there."

I shift her in my arms and hold her close as I walk closer to the well and kick the door open with my foot. You can't really see down too far because that's how I had it built. I don't really like secrets, but some should be kept, and whatever she sees will be of her own choosing, not what's presented.

Children are so innocent at this age. It makes me miss simpler times when I was younger and didn't have to care for anyone other than myself, but I can honestly say that I chose this life because it was the best fit for me.

"Close your eyes," I say to her quickly. She likes to play peek-a-boo, and I'll turn her into a world class fucking champion if that's what she wants. Playing this little game right now will also lessen the blow of what she might see.

When the sun is at its peak like it is right now, you can almost see all the way down to the bottom.

Almost.

I don't go down there, but before I decided I wanted to keep my baby safe from all the bullshit lies, I did manage to buy and throw some barrels of hay into the well. I figure it was a small act of kindness; a creature comfort for having to stay in a place like that.

I'm not afraid of the oubliette, I'm just better than being reduced to having to stay there, is all.

"Ready?" I say, poking her gently in the stomach.

She lets out a giddy giggle as she peeks through her chubby little fingers and smiles at me, "Yeah!"

"Oh! I can see you peeking!" I say to her playfully. She giggles again and covers her eyes completely. "Alright, baby girl. On three. Ready? One ... Two ... Two and a half ..." she giggles again, and I can't help but laugh. Pulling her close, I give her a kiss on the side of her head before I finish my countdown, "Three! Open your eyes and look!"

She quickly pulls her hands away and leans so far over that I have to adjust her again to keep her from falling.

"Hi Mama!" she calls out.

I can hear the hay shifting slightly, but there's no response.

"Hey! She's talking to you!" I call down sharply. "Say hi!"

The same sound of the rustling needles greets my ears and I sigh.

"Mama's tired right now, baby girl. She'll be okay to talk to you tomorrow. Is that alright?"

"Bye Mama!" she calls out again.

I guess it is.

I use my foot to close the lid again, then place her back down onto the grass. I cross my arms loosely over my chest, and laugh as she takes off running, squealing happily at the top of her lungs.

I'll never replace Jocelyn as my true wife. I can't; that girl has meant more to me than any other wife before her, and she's helped me a lot too, in the emotional sense. She showed me that I *can* be a better person, and when I still feel the need for physical contact, I toss the ladder down into the well so I can fuck her.

It's probably why she's still alive, too. Being able to fuck her keeps my mind straight on being a father and not the evil bastard she thinks I am. Maybe one day I'll let her out permanently, and we can raise this one together, but I doubt it.

If she knew the little collection of wasted wives I kept in my special rooms that she's so damn scared of, she'd know that being down in the hole is better than being above ground for her.

I can't help but shake my head and chuckle.

A few years ago, when that couple came back to get their damn dog, she spilled every single fucking secret we had, so of course I had to kill them. I didn't want to, but she forced my hand. The best part is that no one ever came looking for them. There were no missing persons alerts in the newspapers or in the media.

I found out later on that they were drifters. They never ended up renting the house next door; they just wanted someone to watch their dog while they found a new place to squat.

Fucking losers.

All of them.

Laura. Vaughn. Eloy.

But I guess it's safe to say that a wasted fuck, leads to a waste of children, with the exception of my sweet Joce. God, just thinking about her down in the darkness, dirty, alone, scared, is enough to make me wanna throw the ladder down for a quick fuck, but I can't today.

I promised my baby girl I'd take her to the zoo, and since I'm damn determined to be a good fucking parent, that's what we're gonna do.

I'm going to honor him. I'm going to ensure that his legacy lives on. – Hailey Chazen

Maelstrom:

Pre-order by scanning here:

Grab your FREE copy of What Lies
Beneath by scanning here:

*"The atmosphere is dark and
ominous, and there's seemingly no
escape from the monster. But the
question is, who is the real monster?"*
– USA Today Bestselling Author
Ellie Midwood

ABOUT THE AUTHOR

Yolanda Olson is a USA Today Bestselling and award-winning author. Born and raised in Bridgeport, CT where she currently resides, she usually spends her time watching her favorite channel, Investigation Discovery. Occasionally, she takes a break to write books and test the limits of her mind. Also an avid horror movie fan, she likes to incorporate dark elements into the majority of her books.

View Yolanda's books by scanning here:

Printed in Great Britain
by Amazon